## About the Author

Ingrid Lynch is a retired teacher. Her favorite students were those solid C kids who did their best and defended the bullied. They were always champions! She writes about those thought to be losers who turn out to be winners. And, yes, usually there's at least one dog (or more) in her stories.

# Love's Champion

# Ingrid Lynch

# Love's Champion

Olympia Publishers
*London*

**www.olympiapublishers.com**
OLYMPIA PAPERBACK EDITION

A CIP catalogue record for this title is
available from the British Library.

ISBN: 978-1-80074-951-1

This is a work of fiction.
Names, characters, places and incidents originate from the writer's
imagination. Any resemblance to actual persons, living or dead, is
purely coincidental.

First Published in 2023

Olympia Publishers
Tallis House
2 Tallis Street
London
EC4Y 0AB

Printed in Great Britain

# Dedication

For Drollene Brown, who always took time from her busy editor
business to show me I must put "clothes" on sentence skeletons.

On a quiet and hot summer day, Marvin Dorset sat at the Verde Diner, waiting for three of his childhood friends to join him for lunch. It was something they often did on Wednesdays. Later, after that lunch, he would think to himself how things might have turned out differently if he hadn't paid such sharp attention to Shaggy's comment about Ron rubbing his legs. Shaggy often said crazy things, and what she said always turned out to be right on the money. Ron had been his best friend ever since they were toddlers, so what she said bothered him, considering what he'd heard about Ron lately.

Marvin's dusty deputy vehicle was parked outside the diner, along with all the farmers' pickups and trucks, much different from the snappy Jaguar convertible Ron Gesler owned. Ron lived in a huge place filled with expensive furnishings, the son of a glamorous mother and a man who had inherited family businesses.

Marvin, on the other hand, was the son of a Cherokee father and a white mother. Ellen Fitzgerald's family had disowned her after she moved in with Frank Dorset. The fact she was pregnant with Marvin before she and Frank married was too much for them. And yet, Ellen had been supremely happy in their humble home, where the three people there were more important than the sparse furniture. Even when Marvin was a little boy, when he was with Ron in Ron's home, he could certainly tell it was possessions that counted with Ron's mom, Tressa; the two mothers were very different.

Geraldine, the Geslers' housekeeper, would drop off little Ron at the Dorsets' home, and the two boys would play with trucks and cars and Spider Man in Marvin's room or under the big walnut tree out in front of Frank's home. Sometimes, at school or elsewhere, Marvin heard an old taunt: "Apple, Apple,

Indian—red on the outside, white on the inside." It never bothered him, for even as they became teenagers, Ron and Marvin, along with Joe Anders and Cal Peterson and his brothers, worked on their cars and on Frank's old tractor together, and they walked into each other's kitchens without even knocking.

Some things were accepted because they were true and immutable: Ron's father, Hal, was a drunk and Marvin's mom died. These were things the two boys dealt with as best they could. Ron tried every way he could to please his critical father. Marvin became very defensive of his father, Frank, for he knew well the sorrow that never was discussed.

Probably it was his mother's death when he was so young that made Marvin a quiet, introspective young man, always protective, never missing anything. The people of Verde felt Marvin was pretty much their detective. If the police needed anything better, they could call on nearby Rosemont or the larger city of Steeds.

He'd been born in Verde and lived all his life in this pleasant place. His opinion was that the world held all sorts of remarkable things and interesting places, but this one spot was best. He was well read; he loved reading. But what was most important to him was that he was well thought of. And there was productive and protective work to do. Right here, in Verde.

Next to him, lying on a chair, was his wide-brimmed, beat-up, summer straw hat. People said if Marvin put his hat on, slow like, or took it off that way, something of importance was about to be discussed, but if he whipped a hat off or slapped it on, then he was upset. Since he was so cautious about words, folks thought his hats did some of the talking for him.

If he had wanted to, he could step outside the diner and see where his three friends spent a lot of their time. Ron's sister,

Thalia, and Joe Anders' sister, Emma, spent a lot of time at the Gesler Realty office just down the street. Both Thalia and Emma had attended community college along with Marvin. He had become one of Chief Davis's four Verde deputies after those two years. Emma had become a CPA, and Thalia had become a real estate agent. The two women worked together, trying to salvage some of the Gesler businesses in these hard times.

The town of Verde and all the farms surrounding it had been experiencing two and a half long years of drought and lowered expectations. It was hard scrabble for everybody. The little Puncheon River, which wound through town, was at its lowest level ever. It was polluted by fertilizer run-off from the farms and by the tomato cannery upriver. Some farmers close to the river were irrigating fields from it, but most farms, not having that irrigation, were suffering. It was just not the best of summers.

Across the street, Marvin could see the office of the local newspaper, *The Guardian*, where his friend Margaret, better known as Shaggy, worked as a copy editor. Shaggy had attended community college along with Marvin and the other two. Much of Shaggy's time lately, though, was taken up with Joe Anders. She'd married Joe, and together they'd been managing their two adjoining farms, but Joe was sick now. Marvin knew Emma and Shaggy were worried, because nobody could figure out what was wrong with Joe.

People were surprised when Shaggy married Joe, because growing up, Marvin was always wherever Shaggy was. That began when they were small children, when a sudden storm drove those two along with other kids into somebody's screened porch. Shaggy ended up huddled at the end of the porch swing, hanging onto the swing chain. When lightning hit a nearby tree, electricity ran down the tree trunk, throwing bark against the porch screen—*splat, splat*—and then it leapt onto that swing chain. An electrified Shaggy had been hurled out of the swing, across the porch, through the screen into a snowball bush, where Marvin found her, lying dazed.

After that, he looked after her, for she was so small, and so many things happened to her. Another storm had broken part of a willow tree down, so that it was still attached to the trunk but was now spread to the ground, making of itself a natural sliding board in Shaggy's eyes.

"Oh," she had said, "there's hornets in this tree, and they're mad, and they're gonna sting somebody!" That "somebody" turned out to be Shaggy, with so many stingers in her behind (for she had been sliding down the tree trunk backwards), she ended up in the doctor's office.

Only a few days after that, Marvin and she had been sitting on the grass outside the church, waiting their turn to practice their parts for the traditional Children's Day, a Sunday when all the church children sang songs or recited something. Shaggy had suddenly announced, "You know, Georgie's teasing his dog, and now he's mad, and he's gonna bite somebody!" It seemed to Marvin it was almost immediately after that, here came George Royce and a friend running as fast as they could go for the church side door. They were pursued by a very angry chow-chow dog. The two boys ran inside the church, and, because they were afraid of the dog, they refused to open the door to let Shaggy and Marvin in. Marvin was fighting the dog, but Shaggy ran off, her little legs pumping as she rounded the corner of the church. The dog immediately ran after her.

Marvin ran behind them both, yelling, "Stop running, Shaggy! Stop running!" The dog was jumping up and biting her on her behind as she ran. When she finally stopped running, the

12

confused dog ran home.

And Shaggy ended up in the doctor's office again. This time, the doctor suggested to Shaggy's mom her little girl should start wrecking some other parts of her body.

The following week she fell out of Frank's walnut tree and broke her arm.

Marvin, as he sat in the diner sipping his coffee, waiting for his friends, could well remember being in Ron's kitchen, enjoying Geraldine's cookies, asking her about Shaggy.

"How come she knew about those hornets, Geraldine?" he'd asked. "How come Shaggy knew Georgie had been pitchin' his pocketknife between his dog's legs, makin' him mad like that, huh?"

Geraldine hadn't been very sympathetic. "Harrumph! If she's so smart, how come Shaggy is always the one getting hurt all the time?"

That day Marvin got a glimpse of what life was really like for Ron and his sister Thalia, even way back then, as Lou, the handyman for the Geslers, had come complaining into the kitchen. Marvin remembered well what Lou had said.

"He's always out there drunk, Geraldine, picking on his kids and talkin' down his wife! I'm trying to get things done, and there he is! He picks on his little girl because she looks like the missus, I think. Somebody ought to beat some sense into him!"

"You out there gettin' him drunk so he can't even hobble into the house, are you?"

"Nah, nah, nah, Geraldine, nah. He's drunk when he gets here."

As Marvin sat nursing his coffee, he was unhappily wondering how Lou was getting along now, today, in Steeds, where he had found him at a homeless shelter. Geraldine hadn't reported it, but Thalia had, asking him to see if he could find Lou, a runaway from home, so to speak. Lou had traveled with a trucker weeks and weeks ago. He'd been hit by a car at an intersection, breaking his leg. When the hospital released him, he had no place to go, but he sure wasn't interested in going back to Geraldine.

"Don't you imagine Geraldine misses you?" Marvin had tried.

That didn't work. "She won't miss me no more than bird crap in a bird's nest," Lou had countered. "I can't stand it anymore, trying to work there, him always drunk. Been that way for so long. Now, he's takin' to resting his elbow on some ax he's got planted on the ground. He leans on the head of that, always sittin' there at the shed, looking at the back of the house, seeing if Tressa's back at the house, her car there. Gives me the creeps. I tell Geraldine, plenty of jobs in Texas, but she's never leaving that place. Thinks she's the queen of it. I'm staying here."

He meant it. Marvin had to leave Lou there in Steeds, and that was troublesome, for Marvin could sense how in some ways Lou and Geraldine were what held things together at the Gesler place.

And now there was an unusual death that had Marvin puzzled. He figured the young woman who'd been killed must have been a prostitute. Her body was found in the weeds at the truck stop. The top part of her was fully clothed. Bottom part had on only her skimpy panties. No shoes, either. It was strange.

His talk with Lou had been yesterday, and he'd been with Dr. Stevens in Rosemont, too, for the autopsy report on the young woman's body. Yes, there had been sex. It was the head injury that killed her, and she'd been in a fight of some sort, too, for there were bruises.

And there was this expensive-looking piece of jewelry found in a pocket of her jacket. Marvin had viewed the body, and he was not in the best of moods today. He had the necklace with him to see if Shaggy could offer some help from the newspaper, and later he'd take it to jewelers in Rosemont and Steeds to see if they recognized it. A photograph of it would help, if the newspapers would publish it.

He wished those three women would come... and why wouldn't it rain?

Emma was the first to arrive, wearing jeans, sneakers, and a pink short-sleeved top. Yet, whenever he saw her, Marvin always mentally put her with laces and ribbons in something else, for she looked, like her mother, Regina—Reegie—so very French, so very feminine. At one time, Marvin had thought of asking Emma for a date, but he realized her kind of beauty terrified him.

Like Marvin, she'd lost a parent at an early age. Her father had died in a farming accident. But she and her brother, Joe, had reacted to that by making sure every aspect of their lives, every piece of equipment, every possibility of a problem would be met with calm assurance. It was one thing to admire them both but quite another to put himself in a spot where he would know how inferior he was to them. Emma was a dating impossibility. He felt she was the sort of person who would reveal her deepest emotions in a journal.

"Impossible" for dating him meant just about everybody else. Marvin had dated one young woman, and that turned into a catastrophe as soon as she saw how small their farm was and how poor his father and he were. He "postponed" dating, preferring to feel he was as acceptable as anyone else, considering how hard his father and he worked. He realized some females might think it was odd that he and Frank ignored the TV set in the living

15

room, instead favoring the TV in the kitchen, since that was where they usually were. If you turned the porch chairs around backwards and had the back door open, in the summer you could sit on the porch of an evening and by looking through two doorways watch that kitchen TV set. He figured their masculine habits might not be appreciated. Towels were sometimes left lying about, and toilet seats were always left up. Not impressive.

The fact that he was one of the handsomest men in Verde didn't impress him. Tall, with dark hair and eyes, he was an exotic combination of Ellie's Scottish ancestors and Frank's Cherokee folks. He accepted being different, but being handsome didn't matter much to Marvin.

"You want some coffee? Can get you some," he said to Emma. "Are Shaggy and Thalia coming, too?"

"I talked to Shaggy on the phone, and yes, she's coming. Thalia, I can't be sure. She left the office, said she'd be a little late. She wanted to drop by her house to check on Ron. I think she's worried about him. No, no coffee. I had coffee earlier. Maybe some tea with lunch."

"What's going on with Ron, then? Listen, he was gone for a year, and it's been almost three and a half now he's back, and I've seen him to talk to... maybe a few minutes each time... just a few times, and he's not the same, somehow. The whole time he was gone, I never heard a word from him."

Then he remembered how Ron had once looked at Emma, how Emma had once looked at Ron, and how time hadn't been kind to them. He wished he'd kept his mouth shut.

Her face revealed nothing. "Me, neither," she said softly.

Perhaps she would write about Ron in her journal, Marvin thought to himself.

Thalia, at that very moment, was softly traveling down the wide central hall of her home toward the back of the house. Years ago, she had moved her sleeping quarters to the office on the first floor, near the entrance of the house. There was a safe in the office, and there was a lock on the door, so she felt safe sleeping there. She was headed from there to the first-floor master bedroom where now only her mother, Tressa, occasionally slept. Tressa was seldom home, for she spent most of her time in Rosemont at her antique sales and restoration shop. She had an apartment there. Hal Gesler had been banned from sleeping with his wife for some time now. Since that bedroom was empty almost all the time, Thalia was pretty sure her brother was sleeping there.

She wasn't sure how long ago it had been she'd heard a hub-bub of noise and shouting that woke her in the middle of the night. Had it been more than a week ago? It didn't last long enough to keep her awake, though it certainly was loud for a while. Ron always parked his convertible at the rear of the house, and in the past, he'd always used the outside staircase that led to the second-floor landing and doorway. That door was never locked, and, once inside it in the hall, Ron's bedroom was just inside that door.

Since he'd started drinking so heavily, he chose to sleep in Tressa's room instead of going upstairs. Was it possible he was drunk, and he'd tried to get up that outside staircase and fell? And Geraldine, alerted, had come to help him? It wasn't like him to be sleeping so late, in the first place. Ever since she'd heard all that noise, things had gotten worse about Ron.

Now, when she peeked into the bedroom, at first, she thought Tressa must have come home in the middle of the night as she sometimes did. It certainly looked like her blond head on the pillow. It startled her and made her go back into the hall to peer out the back door, looking to see if Tressa's car was parked somewhere out there. Only Ron's vintage white Jaguar convertible was there.

A closer inspection of Tressa's room showed Thalia it was Ron, asleep, wearing one of his mother's wigs. Who knew what a drunken Ron thought was funny? She was troubled as she quietly closed the bedroom door. She left the house from the front entrance to join her friends at the diner.

Shaggy arrived next with two dogs. She had no business entering a diner with two Great Dane puppies, but that was what she did. She came looking like a teenager, if you saw her from the rear. Wearing jeans and sneakers, like Emma, but wearing a work shirt, sleeves rolled up. It was when you saw her face you'd realize this was an adult woman wearing no makeup, one who let time and nature do whatever they wanted to. It was one of the things Marvin liked most about Shaggy. Her fly-away hair was in a long plait hanging down her back. She had the two rollicking dogs on show leads rather than regular leashes, and she was getting jerked about, to the amusement of the diners who were watching.

Everyone in the place knew Shaggy's big Great Dane bitch, Skittles, had puppies, and these must be two of them. Some people had critical things to say about Shaggy, trying to sell huge purebred dogs in hard times. They wondered how Joe put up with her. But most of the diners were smiling and liked seeing the dogs.

One was black with distinctive white face markings, and the other was larger, that traditional tawny Dane color, with black ears and face. He would grow to be a royal sort of dog. Like teenagers who don't know for sure where their feet end when they grow so fast, they were trying to be playful but were sprawling, pawing at each other, ears flopping over—when those ears should be straight up.

"Don't you say no, now, Emma! This shiny black girl is for you, and she'll be company for you when you're alone out there on your farm all day, and I know that, see. Your mom is over at our place helping out with Joe nearly every day. I have the puppy's papers right here in my purse. She has an AKC name, but you get to name her anything you want her to be called." Shaggy started digging in her purse.

Marvin saw Emma frown for a moment, and he was afraid she'd say no to the dog, but then she looked as if she were aware of how hard it was for Shaggy to get rid of those big puppies. He thought her face reflected a kind thought for her sister-in-law, Shaggy. *What are good friends for, anyway?* he supposed Emma must be thinking, as she nodded yes.

She took the lead from Shaggy's hand. They sat side-by-side, looking at the papers, heads together, talking. Well, it was as if that dog still would be Shaggy's, for the two farms were adjoined, Joe's old home farm where now Emma lived alone so much of the time and Shaggy's family place where Joe lived now with her.

"I'll have to tape the ears, so they stand up as they get older," Shaggy was explaining, and that was when Thalia arrived.

Marvin's heart always skipped when he saw her. His was a constant concern for her, something he felt but never fully understood. It was as if he sensed she was alone somehow.

She was as beautifully blond and blue-eyed as her mother Tressa, wearing blue slacks with colorful flats and a white blouse, tucked in. Very simple and understated. He was wondering what he could say to her, but at that moment Shaggy saw her and began her pitch to Thalia about the second puppy.

"You mustn't say no. Geraldine will love this dog! He's going to be a show dog—so gorgeous!" Then she leaned closer, her voice more pleading, "Thalia, I picked this male out especially for you…"

Her voice trailed off, and for a moment, Shaggy looked confused. She touched Thalia's hair, saying to her, "This is so dumb, but for a moment there, Thalia, I thought you were wearing a wig." Thalia was stunned, as Shaggy corrected herself, "No, no, not that. You were *thinking* about a wig. That's it, isn't it?"

Thalia looked as if she'd seen a snake. But she composed herself quickly.

"For God's sake, Shaggy. You always shock me. Remember when you said in school Miss Gertrude's washing machine wasn't working right?"

"She was *thinking* that!"

"And later on, we found out she had a new washing machine!"

"Yeah, right."

But Shaggy wasn't done. "Why was Ron rubbing his legs? Thalia, why was Ron doing that?"

Thalia didn't seem to have heard her. "I've been *thinking* about buying a wig," Thalia lied. "Think I should?"

"No, not really. It would look tacky."

Their talk went on during lunch, with the two puppies, still at last, lying on the floor sprawled between the legs of their humans.

After lunch Thalia needed to go back into the office to look at some maps, make a few phone calls. There was some German company interested in buying land near Verde. But now she added, "I'll have to get this fellow here situated where he'll be safe and happy. And I'll get some supplies. Be thinking of a good name for him!" She led the dog to the door, and he went willingly with her.

"He's going to be a champion," Shaggy told her.

At the door she stopped and looked back at Shaggy, a look that caught Marvin's breath.

"Oh, Shaggy," she said softly, "I've always wanted a champion."

Marvin fought the urge to stand and say, "Champion volunteer here!" Then he realized he'd said not one word to her all during their lunch. Later, he would look in the mirror at himself and wonder if she had any idea he fancied himself to be her champion. What he saw was a face he felt was a regular sort, but it was a rugged, western face that looked back at him from the mirror. His eyes were so brown they were almost black, with dark eyelashes and eyebrows. He had a straight nose and dark, straight hair and was taller than his father and most of the fellows he knew. He looked a lot like an Indian but with a strong touch of his mother's whiteness. He never thought of himself as being handsome—and he never felt "Marvin" sat well on him as a name.

It was after Thalia and the male puppy left that Marvin remembered the favor he wanted to ask of Shaggy. He took out the necklace. "This is something the newspaper can photograph, and then I'm hoping the paper will publish it," he explained to Shaggy. "Somebody might recognize it. I guess you've heard about the death of that young woman. This has to do with that. Think you could ask, Shaggy?"

Emma looked at it with interest. Shaggy not so much, because she was celebrating, inwardly, the fact there was now only one puppy left at home, and perhaps she could keep that one. With relief, she was thinking of ordering a dessert.

She glanced at the necklace. "Sure I can," she said, "and I'm sure they would photograph it, too, but you don't have to do that. Emma, remember? Tressa had guests at her shop to look at some big estate's antiques, and she wore that. The necklace belongs to Tressa."

Thalia was in a good mood as she traveled home, not just because of the puppy on the passenger seat beside her, but also because when she had stopped at the office to return the phone call from Norfunt, the news from them was encouraging. The German company was seeking an American location for a plant they would build. It would have to be flat, close to trucking and rail and air lines. And Norfunt wanted a rural setting for cheap labor. Thalia knew her family enterprises were a mess, but their orchards were still producing income, and some farmers were paying a little at a time on what they owed because they'd made some money from winter wheat. Others had it so much harder. She knew a plant and the jobs it offered might be a very good thing for her little town.

Now, at her home, she took the smaller drive, the straight one that broke away from the wide sweeping driveway leading to the back of the house. The small driveway led to the front of the house. She parked there at the front entrance. If her father were around, he would be sitting at the garden shed, just as he always did when Lou had to put up with him, and he would have seen her if she parked out back. She wanted to keep the dog a secret from him, at least for the moment. Right now, she wanted to introduce the dog to Geraldine.

The big puppy kept up with her as she went down the

hallway toward the kitchen, his padded feet moving silently, one ear up properly, the other impudently flopping. When Geraldine saw the big dog, she gave a little cry of alarm, which caused him to step back, but he quickly recovered his dog wits about him.

"He's here to stay," Thalia said firmly.

"What will Tressa say?" Geraldine wanted to know, rolling her eyes. "All her rugs and antiques here." It was Tressa who owned those treasures, but it was Geraldine who had to care for them. A dog was going to mean extra work.

"I'm counting on Ron." When Thalia said that, Geraldine nodded, for both of them knew that so far as she was able to show any affection, Tressa loved her son. If Ron wanted the dog to stay, it probably would.

"I'll keep him with me most of the time, and I'll include him in the front office. It'll be his place and mine. I'll feed him there, water him there, sleep there with him, so he won't whine. If once in a while you have to take him for short periods of time, Geraldine, put him in the laundry room. I don't want him outside loose. Not loose, and never, never near the garden shed. He could be hurt there. Okay?"

The housekeeper nodded yes, understanding Hal was a danger and also because her twice-a-month check came from Thalia's efforts, not anyone else's.

"I'm going to take him with me to get his supplies now before the pet supply store closes, but I'll be back. If you see Ron, tell him I want to talk to him. Let him know about the dog, will you?"

When Thalia left, Geraldine sat for a bit, possibly wondering what life would be like with something so big in the laundry room. He probably wasn't housebroken yet, she thought to herself. She bet he would pee in that laundry room.

23

She was still sitting there when Ron, finally awake and dressed, came into the kitchen. He intended to tell Geraldine to leave some dinner for him in the refrigerator, that he would be changing clothes and going out for the evening, possibly all night. Even when not fully awake, Ron was, like his sister, favored by Geraldine, "mothered" by her.

"You're in for a surprise," Geraldine said, and she told him about the dog. At first, Ron wasn't interested, until she remarked that it was the biggest puppy she ever saw.

"What? What kind of dog is it?" he asked, and when she told him it was one of those Great Dane dogs and Thalia would be back and wanted to talk to him, he sat up straight. Yes, and the dog would be having the front office as his room, and it was up to him to square things with his mother about this dog.

Maybe he wouldn't go out after all, he decided.

At the store, where they had all kinds of pet food and supplies, the staff exclaimed enthusiastically over the Dane puppy. "Oh, it's one of Skittle's pups! This one is going to be majestic! He's huge already!"

Thalia came out of the store with a giant bag of puppy food, another bag of expensive dog food—this one for the adult dog—directions for feeding, a water dish, a food dish, the biggest dog bed she ever saw, and the phone number for the vet the staff recommended. "You're expensive already," she said accusingly to the dog, as she drove away.

She didn't want her father to harm this dog. She learned when she had just turned six years old what her father had become. He was angry because she'd worn her best clothes at her birthday party and gotten them all dirty when she and her playmates were running around in the garden after her party ended. When he saw she was alone in the garden the next day, he

24

came lurching out of the house pulling her little red wagon with her party dress and shoes in it. Slurring insults, he'd thrown the wagon and her dress and shoes into the Puncheon River, which flowed past the Gesler home, and he'd added, as he stumbled away, a suggestion she should go into the river herself and drown.

She'd been small then, but she'd noticed how her parents were warring against each other, and so she never spoke of what had happened. Meals were hellish, with her mother doting on her son, Ron, and Hal drunk and insulting to both his children and his wife.

It was when she was eleven her father's attack became physical. Her mother was so seldom home, a lonely Thalia had spotted Tressa's black velvet bedroom slippers beside the bed in the master bedroom, and she ventured into the room intent on slipping her little foot into one of Tressa's slippers.

She didn't know her father had come into the room behind her. There were no words spoken. She was picked up and thrown onto the bed. It was so frightening, her arms and legs were already flailing about as she landed, and she bounced off the bed and ran past him out the door he'd left open. She'd fled up and across the hall to the safety of the kitchen and Geraldine.

This time, she did speak of it to her mother. She chose to tell Tressa about it in the kitchen with Geraldine present. It had shocked her when she saw how her mother responded.

"Oh, for Heaven's sakes, grow up!" she said to her eleven-year-old. "He's an idiot drunk! You and Geraldine have to handle this!"

"But you're my mom! You should be here! You're never *here*!"

On Tressa's hand, a large diamond ring flashed, as she drummed her fingers impatiently on the kitchen table.

"Well, I'm not," came the frosty reply.

From then on, Thalia became increasingly aware her beautiful mother didn't want a younger look-alike daughter anywhere near her. Thalia's bedroom (until she changed it) was second floor, front of the building, while her mother's was first floor, rear. Thalia learned to accept she was, in a sense, an orphan. Hating her parents was useless, so instead, she tried missing them, pretending they were off somewhere and would be back.

Her brother, Ron, dated and went to the prom. She did not.

She had come into her own when she discovered she had a good head on her shoulders for business, for figuring, like her grandfather, knowing every dollar advantage and how to get it.

She was surprised to see Ron sitting on the front steps when she returned and learn he'd already talked to Tressa. The dog was fine, as long as it didn't move around the rest of the house.

And could he please walk the dog a little, he asked, here along the driveway? While he did that, Thalia looked inside the front office, and she was surprised to see a cot there, alongside the bed Geraldine long ago had helped Thalia set up for herself. He'd probably gotten the cot from a storage closet in one of the guest rooms upstairs.

"Why the cot?" she asked him.

That cot, Ron said, was for the dog to sleep on, and the bed was for Ron to use for sleeping. She managed to choke back any objections. She offered him the dog bed and all the other supplies.

She would feel a sudden rush of love for her brother when, late in the evening, she looked in to see the dog and man were sleeping on the twin bed together. The cot had disappeared. The expensive dog bed was ignored. There was a possessive arm over the dog, and Ron's head was resting on its neck as both slept. Ron had named *his* dog Scrambler.

Well, just as well, for she had a lot to discuss with Emma about Norfunt. She considered sleeping at the Realty Office or at Emma's, at least for a while. Instead, she settled for the room across the hall from the office. Ron was nearby; should be safe there.

At the diner, Shaggy was trying to talk Marvin into accepting the very last puppy. He wasn't going for it.

"I wish I knew what to say to convince you," she told him.

He was mentally chewing on the news the necklace was Tressa's and there was that remark about Ron rubbing his legs. "I'm thinking you've already said enough, Margaret," he said, irritated, calling her by her given name. Life was too complicated for Marvin today.

She'd opened the large envelope eagerly. Thalia had been sure a European company would be a welcome relief for drought-stricken farmers. Now she could see Norfunt was a bigger deal than she thought. They would require a railroad spur, some rail access right up to their loading platform. If the rail line was close enough, they would pay to build a spur line to their loading platforms. So their land purchase had to be close to working rail lines. Ditto for truck routes; there had to be a large parking/loading area for trucks. There would be an office building, the large factory itself, and a warehouse building with another loading platform. Norfunt had done some searching on topographical maps, and they'd picked a site they were interested in. However, they wanted an explanation for an area at the very center of that site, something labeled "Cher." They wanted some explanation of that. She thought that would mean Frank Dorset's place. Their suggested site would include Dorset, part of the

27

Petersons' three holdings, and just about half of Shaggy's and Reegie's farms.

That wasn't all. They intended to invite a real estate company to buy up adjoining farms. They thought housing would be a good idea, since their presence (at least in Europe) stimulated the local economy, including the housing market. Of course, the company would profit from all this development, just as the locals would.

This was going to take some convincing, Thalia could see.

Emma wasn't so sure she could help convince anyone their land should be sold. Certainly not her brother, Joe, who was so sick. And she wouldn't have any opinion that counted with Cal Peterson and his brothers, those whose three large farms made up the largest landholdings in the area. Well, nothing was all that certain about this land sale to the Germans, anyway. Maybe nothing would come of it all.

Emma had no reservations about taking back the name Anders after her divorce from Cal Peterson, but she did have some regrets about the breakup. She certainly hadn't been thinking of Cal when she had her fling with Ron Gesler.

Cal and his brothers were all tall and handsome. They had winning smiles and were sincerely well liked. People said those three had higher moral values than most preachers. If she were asked to describe Calvin with one word, Emma thought she probably would say "confident."

When Ron went off to Chapel Hill, Cal was quick to come courting. He was constant in his attention to her when Marvin, Shaggy, Thalia, and she attended community college, and he hung on with his courting even when she went on to get her CPA degree. She'd married him happily. She hadn't been thinking of

Ron Gesler that day, but later on, he crept into her thoughts.

Why had she felt Ron was being punished in some way and that he was unable to help himself? If she had to choose one word to describe Ron, she knew she would have said "lost." Before he went off to college, she could tell Ron was attracted to her. There was that softness in the way he looked at her or touched her hand.

An entirely different Ron returned a year or so later. It was as if the Ron she knew had the life sucked out of him. He was constantly with his father, running with the wrong people, doing the wrong things. He didn't call, and after they were all working, back home, and she and Cal married, Ron probably didn't even notice.

But as time passed, Ron began to come in often when she sat in Tressa's antique shop in Rosemont, balancing the books and checking accounts every sixth month or so, whenever Tressa wanted her there. Emma had no office; she went to clients and worked at their locations.

Ron would get some coffee for both of them, sit and talk with her, as if nothing had changed, as if there was some unfinished business between them that needed to be attended to.

The thing they both knew was on their minds had happened on an ordinary day when they went together to a hotel. They spent that afternoon and most of the evening together, parting just in time to escape Cal's detection. She had been bedded by Cal many times, and there was nothing in her relationship with him that could compare with that one time with Ron. That was a one-time experience that would be, must be, left untouched, wisely never repeated. She felt no guilt or remorse about it.

A few days after that memorable afternoon and evening, Emma sat on the porch with a glass of sweet tea, and she was honest with her husband. He took what she told him stoically, but his eyes grew wide with shocked amazement: first, that she could possibly prefer someone like Ron over him, and second, that she could be so calm when she spoke to him about it. How could she have let that happen? She didn't know how to explain to him that he, Cal, had been blessed in so many ways by so many things. How could he understand her need to tend to someone she felt had been battered and cursed?

He retreated, of course. There wasn't any anger, but he closed his heart against her. She gathered her things and left his family farm, going back to her own home place, to the farm where she and Joe had grown up.

Some men don't become angry or threatening when they're hurt, and they don't cry or spout accusations. Cal Peterson, usually open and honest, quietly moved into a hurt silence.

Emma was firm. "I don't want to ask Cal for anything," she said. "I caused the divorce to happen. It was my fault, not his." She was truthful with her mother.

"Well, it happened," was Reegie's reply. "We got over your father's death. We can handle this."

"You think Cal and his brothers will still help Joe when he needs it? Joe could get worse." Emma knew Reegie was concerned for Joe most of all.

"Cal still comes to help. So far, anyway. He won't hold anything against Joe. And you have that CPA degree. It'll all work out. Chin up, dear." Reegie was saddened by the divorce, but she wasn't a mother who stopped loving a child who'd shown poor judgment.

There was nothing for Emma to expect from either Cal or Ron, but the farm expected a lot. These were hard times, and with Joe so sick, sometimes it was Cal or his brothers who came to help, and Reegie spent most of her time at Shaggy's, helping with

Joe. That meant Emma often had to handle things at her home farm all by herself.

The black Great Dane with her clown face was a great morale builder, a source of affection and wonder just when those things were most needed. Dogs are enthused by the simplest, sweetly normal things. A lifting mist at dawn is enough to encourage a dog to make a run at it; a caterpillar's movement across the grass causes a dog to stop and inquire of it with an uplifted paw; and the clucking of a hen makes a dog shake its head as if trying to make sense of that conversation. Simplicity can be contagious. Emma named her dog Artemis and called her Arty.

When Emma realized Thalia was serious about land sale to the Germans, she thought of the stories she'd been told about men who committed suicide rather than lose their homes, those farms where they'd been so busy all their lives, where they knew the land so well, and the land knew them. When Arty joined up with Shaggy's young bitch, the one puppy Shaggy kept, the two dogs ran with huge energy. It was hard to imagine them having the land taken from beneath their feet. Did they not have a vote about selling, based on their joy? She thought perhaps they did. She already knew, sooner or later, she was going to have to tell Thalia they wouldn't sell—Shaggy and Joe, and Reegie and she, herself, Emma.

Thalia talked about how, if the sale prices were generous, each family could start over somewhere else, a better place with better conditions. Emma wondered how Thalia would go about getting her mother and father and brother to agree to sell any of their land. She'd heard Ron was a more settled person now that he'd taken over the dog Thalia was given. Now then, how would Ron feel about giving up land?

Emma had seen a happier Ron. On one occasion, she was at Tressa's shop, working, when Ron came in, waving an antique cane he'd appropriated from his mother's stock of old weapons. A twist of the cane's silver top, and out came a flashing blade, catching the sun from the windows behind Ron.

"Look!" he cried, "some dude back in the Middle Ages had this!" It was that dimpled boyish quality that made men so attractive, Emma decided.

"It's not as old as you seem to think," Tressa said, "and no, you can't have it." But she was smiling.

"Well, then, I'm borrowing it," he responded.

Recently, Emma had been with Thalia when they stopped at her house to get some papers needed for a meeting at the orchards. When Emma saw Ron walking his huge dog, she got out of the car and joined him. They walked down the longer driveway that swung out in a half circle before it turned to the back of the house.

Thalia had gone into the house to retrieve the needed papers. Ron was relaxed, smiling. "You know," he said, "I used to come roaring along this driveway after working on cars all afternoon— made so much noise everyone for miles around could probably hear me—and then I'd sleep like a baby. Maybe I can work on cars again, you think?"

Emma agreed that was possible, and then she asked him, "Are you and I at peace with one another, now, these days?"

He gave her a gentle smile. "Yeah, we are." But he wouldn't look at her.

Sometimes Emma dreamed about the father she had difficulty remembering. He'd be driving his car, and she'd be a passenger in the back seat. It was at night and scary, for they were passing a cemetery, and over the entrance to it was an iron fretwork that announced, "The Odd Fellows." She wanted to ask her father about the sign, but she didn't. That was because she was warm and safe in the car with him, and she knew he was headed home, where her mother and brother were waiting for them. Then she'd wake up, hearing a comforting rooster crow. So sometimes she felt her father was with her, even though she was alone, that he'd let her know he'd arrived and was tending to things whenever she heard a rooster crow. The memory of that father and how he was still part of the farm was one reason Emma wasn't going to sell.

She heard from others that Cal was saying very little, keeping mostly to himself. She wondered if he had a new love yet, even as she told herself it wasn't any of her business.

Once she was at Joe and Shaggy's farm, helping out, and she came face to face with Cal. She had come out of the hen house with a basket of eggs, and there he was, surprised to see her, she could tell. He stood his ground, though, speaking to her kindly. It was an impersonal conversation. She knew then when two people come apart, split, that each and every second away from each other creates an increasingly deep chasm stretching between them, such a big hole, ever widening, that no one can bridge it or travel across it. No intimacy can ever again be the same... never, never, for a lifetime.

It is the price people pay.

Emma's Journal Entry

*Sometimes when I go get eggs, there's a hen there keeps commenting. Shaggy says she's noticed the same thing. Mom, maybe not. I say, Hello, setting hen, and she says back her hen stuff,* brok, brokbrok. *When I tell her thank you for the eggs, there is more* brok, brok. *But when I tell her times are hard, and if she*

33

*doesn't have eggs, then she's going to end up in the pot and get eaten, then it's different. Then her conversation is* BROK! BROKBROKBROK! BROK! *And they say animals don't understand anything!*

Ron Gesler fervently wished he'd been left alone and never sent off to college. He never was much of a student. He was a fairly good athlete, but his interests were racing and cars, not academic subjects or sports. Starting at about age fifteen, he and the three Peterson brothers and Joe Anders and Marvin, and a few others met at Frank Dorset's place every chance they got, weekends, and all during summers. There they worked on their cars and on Dorset's tractor, which needed attention every so often. He loved life then. Why hadn't he been left alone? Instead, his father got him into Chapel Hill and insisted he go there.

In those days, he still wanted to please his father, so that's what he did. That first day, he stood surrounded and intimidated by everything unfamiliar. He must have been thinking of his budding interest in Emma, because what he remarked to his dad was that this was a strange place, and he didn't know anybody, and he bet he wouldn't even be able to get a date here in this place.

Hal Gesler laughed. "See that dorm over there?" he asked. "That's a women's dorm, and it's full of whores. It's a grocery store, where you can shop any old time you want to."

It turned out that dorm life and fraternity life and party life were satisfying things for Ron. He had a dizzying year of booze and sex, and he didn't do what he should have. There were several consequences: he caught a social disease that needed and got attention; he had a lousy reputation among the females at Chapel Hill; and he flunked out.

Back home, he continued the only thing he'd mastered—the pursuit of pleasure.

Something happened that was unexpected, though. He tired of his father. Hal was showing up for meals fewer and fewer times, and he was staying away for days at a time. Tressa was absent more and more. Hal took to sitting in the doorway of the garden shed out in back, under its jutting roof, chatting with Lou, the handyman. Lately, Lou hadn't been there much, so it was Ron who had to listen to the insulting things Hal was saying about Tressa. Ron tried not to be around, hating to listen to what was being said against his mother, but Geraldine would send him out to inquire about meals, and he would get caught up in it.

It was a comment about Tressa that caused a serious attack. It was Tressa on her broom, riding into Hal's life and making it hell that made his life a misery, Hal was saying. Unwisely, Ron spoke up. He wanted Hal to stop being so cruel about Tressa, his wife and the mother of his children, and now Ron said so.

Ron was sitting in a rickety chair at the garden work shed, looking toward the house when he said that. If he'd been paying attention, he would have seen Hal hoisting the ax that was always at his side into striking position. When Ron turned toward his father, Hal struck his face with the blunt end of the ax, breaking his nose. It also smashed into his mouth, chipping two teeth. It knocked him out of the chair, putting him on the ground,

It not only injured Ron, it frightened him. Hal Gesler was one of those men who had such natural athletic abilities they seemed to remain strong no matter how old they got to be. At that moment, as Ron looked up, he was much afraid of his father

"I'm going out now," Hal said, "but you're not coming with me." And he left.

Ron struggled into the house. Tressa, called into action by

35

Geraldine and Thalia, arrived, enraged. She and Thalia took him to the hospital emergency room. Thalia had done as she was told, making it clear no charges were to be made against her father. Bad for business, Ron supposed. Maybe bad for his mother's antique shop, where genteel people came to buy.

For a long time after that, Ron stuck around the house. He didn't go out in public where people could see his bruised and battered mouth, his taped nose, his darkened eye.

Hal would come sit at the gardening shed and eat what Geraldine prepared and saved for him. Ron stayed away from him. After the dentist and doctors had their healing ways with Ron and time passed, still he preferred having nothing more to do with his father.

Emma's Journal Entry

*I'm wondering why it is Thalia isn't thinking like a real farm woman would think. If you're going to sell, you have to see what you're going to be able to buy and where that is. It's possible no matter how much money you got here, wherever you land, it might not be enough to buy what land is selling for there.*

*Joe got the land ready, even though he's sick, and now Reegie and I have rows and rows of zinnias. So pretty! We talked about Marvin—Joe and I did. Marvin is the handsomest man in the whole town, and maybe even farther—with his dark eyes and hair, and he's so tall, but he doesn't date. Well, except for dating Laurie, and that went nowhere. So I asked Joe if he thought Marvin is a homosexual. Joe got huffy and said no, of course not. Joe said Frank Dorset keeps to that land because his wife's grave is there, for one thing. And of course, Frank is an Indian, and they don't hunger for fancy places. Frank lives close to God and nature, and his house is pretty plain and short on furniture, that is from what Joe could see of it. Joe says he's been on that property lots of times, and that old Frank and Marvin look out for one another. He says Marvin does what he can to keep the property up, but just the same, it's not the kind of home where you would take your girlfriend to watch TV and have some dinner. According to Joe, if you're slow about thinking of yourself, you can just love somebody else too much.*

Marvin puzzled over Tressa's necklace. She hadn't reported it stolen, and surely she'd had it insured. Over in Rosemont he did some checking, talking to people who knew her and had done business with her. He found the jeweler who'd sold her the necklace a few years earlier, and he talked to some people who didn't trust her. This was because some expensive Japanese prints had been put in her shop on commission to be sold, and those disappeared. Tressa said they'd been stolen, but some folks didn't believe that. Insurance money didn't quite smooth suspicious thoughts. He thought of Shaggy's comment about Ron rubbing his legs. And was it possible Tressa didn't even know she was missing a necklace?

If that young hooker had Tressa's necklace (and she did), then she must have been in Tressa's house, Tressa's room. He was remembering how Ron and he used to run, wearing themselves out, first down that long first-floor hallway from front to the back door, to that doorstep, where steps went down to the ground. There was an outdoor staircase, its steps leading up to the second floor, to a landing there and a doorway). Once in that second-floor hallway, there was Ron's bedroom immediately on the left. The second-floor hall led to the front inside stairs going down to the first floor. Oh, how he and Ron used to run that course over and over, up the outside stairs, down the length of the second-floor hall to the front of the house, down the inside stairs, down the first-floor hall to the back of the house to those outside stairs, up those to the second floor until they were exhausted... or until Geraldine called to them to stop that! "And stop it now! At once!"

And where was she, when she did that? Yelling from the window in her bedroom, from that window right over those steps leading to the ground at the back door. Tressa's bedroom was on one side of that first-floor hallway; the laundry room, pantry and Geraldine's room were all on the other side of it, across the hall.

So, Marvin didn't want to talk to Tressa right away. Instead, maybe it was time to talk to Geraldine. He wanted to talk to her about Lou, anyway.

He took his hat off when he went into Geraldine's kitchen.

Just about everybody had observed Marvin's hats. In winter, he favored a time-worn Stetson, but in summer, it was that wide-brimmed once-was-white straw summer hat. Some said he got his hats from those Frank Dorset was throwing out.

Lou came up first of all. "Thalia's been worried about Lou," Marvin said. "Where is he now, do you know?"

"At homeless places in Steeds, far as I know. He just took off. He left this place. No-account. I'm not missing him." But Marvin noticed as she spoke, she was twisting the kitchen towel she was holding.

"You may not need him here, but I'm thinking I do," Marvin replied. "Ron's face, that convinces me I do. Lou might be handy to have here. And it's time for you to tell me some things I need to hear. Shaggy mentioned Ron rubbing his legs, for one thing."

Geraldine's eyes grew large. "She'll fire me."

"I won't let that happen. And I'm not looking to be pressing charges on anything. I'm Ron's friend, whether you know that or not."

"You won't be able to stop her."

"That's what you think. I know I can. She's not living here anymore, is she, really? It's all been up to you and Thalia, right?"

Geraldine reluctantly nodded her agreement with that.

"But she comes here sometimes, sleeps here sometimes, right? When it suits her?"

Geraldine warmed to that subject. "Yes, well, sometimes she comes after she's finished up with her supper, or work or something, and she gets here late, and she sleeps here. And then, next day she's looking to check on all the things she's got here, because they're on display like, not just living furniture. Then maybe she takes something back with her, something somebody wants, for her to sell. Or she unloads something she wants to put in here. Her business is heavy. She does repairs, too. She has breakfast, and then she's gone."

"Well, then, I need to go into her bedroom."

Geraldine frowned.

"I have to do this. She's had something stolen, and I don't think she knows that. Trust me." He got up and crossed the hall. The door was open, and he simply walked in. "I'm going to be mumbling to myself. Don't get upset."

He could see the headboard of the bed was against the far wall, the bed facing the end of the house. Beside the bed on one side was a chair; on the other side was a door. And at the wall nearest the entry door there was a chest of drawers, and on top of that there was a large wooden jewelry chest of some kind. Another set of four doors on the hall wall clearly opened into a closet.

He went first to the door beside the headboard, opened it, saw it was a bathroom. He mumbled to himself, but loud enough

39

for Geraldine to hear, as he walked around the room imagining what might have happened.

"Okay. He's probably shushing her, saying, 'No noise, now. Quiet.' He's not going to take her all the way up to his room. He's going into this room. This unlocked back door so close to your room, Geraldine. You're not sleeping too well with Lou gone, so you'd hear them. Maybe you're onto what he's up to from the first. Probably he's done this more than once."

Geraldine followed behind, listening as Marvin continued to mumble, walking around the room. "He's on this side of the bed. Bathroom side. Autopsy says he's had sex with her, and now he swings his legs over and out of the bed and into the bathroom he goes. I have her on this other side because there's a chair that side, where she has put her clothes. So she hears the shower, maybe. Puts on her panties and top of her outfit. Then she notices the jewelry box."

Marvin moved to the chest of drawers. "If she's been here more than once, she's probably noticed this before." He glanced at Geraldine. "Same one, maybe? More than once?"

She nodded Yes.

"You know her name?"

Now she shook her head No.

"She's got it open, but when she hears the shower turn off, maybe, she just takes something and puts it in her pocket. And she shuts it, because if she leaves it open, he'll know what she's done."

Marvin opened the big jewelry chest. It sprang open in a startling way. From each lower side a tray of jewelry emerged, and at the top, two other trays spread wide. Tressa Gesler's sparkling and expensive collection of fine jewelry was suddenly on display much as it would be shown at a jewelry store.

"No wonder she hasn't missed anything," Marvin whispered to himself.

Geraldine wasn't smiling when he said, "Now we need to talk about what Shaggy said."

Thalia helped Marvin get together with Ron at last. They sat down for a talk that lasted about fifteen minutes, most of that with Ron's eyes downcast. That sent Marvin to Rosemont to talk with the doctor at the Coroner's Office again, and then to Steeds to talk with the dead girl's parents. At least, she wouldn't be buried as some unknown Jane Doe.

On his way back from Steeds the next day, Marvin thought about Tressa and her eyes, so much like Thalia's, but more intense. Tressa's eyes were piercing, rather bold. He had noticed things about people, about eyes, particularly women's eyes. Marvin hadn't had much experience questioning people, but he'd noticed that while men would squint their eyes, or have their eyes downcast—some men would, anyway, if they had a difficult time answering—a woman did a whole different thing. Her eyes would get wider and rounder if she were telling a lie. Marvin thought so, anyway. He remembered seeing two women look one another over, both of them interested in the same man, and he thought that must be like two tigresses taking measure of each other.

One time, he had been talking to a woman, and at his back there was a walkway elevated up to his shoulder height. On it, he could sense someone was walking, because the woman he was talking to fastened her eyes on that person, following that person's progress along the walkway with such joy in her eyes. He knew it must have been someone the woman favored. Women's eyes said it all. It was going to be painful, but he was going to have to talk to Tressa.

The talk with Tressa got postponed the very next day. Maybe Marvin was trying to prepare himself for it, because he was on his second cup of coffee, walking about outside at home, when he came upon a disheveled Lou Potter sleeping in the shed where Frank Dorset kept his tractor. Lou had found a few burlap bags, wrapped them around himself, and was sleeping huddled in a corner. Geraldine had pretended having no concern about this poor raggedy fellow, but Marvin was sure she cared about him, and now here he was, at the Dorset's place, clearly needing help.

Lou knew, of course, summer soon would be winding down. When winter came, what then? After his discharge from the Steeds hospital, he'd hobbled around on his weak leg. It had healed poorly, and he was walking crooked and lopsided, going to homeless shelters and dumpster diving to find things he could eat.

He finally gave up. It had been a truck driver who gave him a ride to Steeds; now it was another truck driver who brought him close to Verde. Lou had struggled at night to get to Frank's place. And now here he was.

Frank and Marvin both agreed he should stay, certainly long enough to get stronger and more confident. Every day, Lou begged to be permitted to stay on forever. He could still work hard, he insisted. He helped Marvin with the day-after-day splitting wood chore.

And after a while, Marvin had him talking about going back to Geraldine.

"I don't want to ask anything from that woman," Lou kept insisting.

"Nobody's asking you to do that," Marvin assured him. They

42

were having a late lunch together, and now Marvin told Lou exactly what he wanted, which was simply be there. Make the two women and Ron feel safer. By the end of that week, Marvin had a tense Lou (warned to keep quiet), ready to go see Geraldine.

She wasn't pleasantly surprised. "No, not having him here," she said firmly. "He walked out on us."

"I need for him to be here, Geraldine, to help keep Thalia safer, Ron safer, you, yourself, safer. Please now, be reasonable." It was finally agreed Lou could sleep on a cot or in one of the guest bedrooms.

And, so, at last, weeks after he had planned to go talk to Tressa Gesler, Marvin was actually going to have to do so. On an early Friday morning, a day promising to be just as hot as the previous day had been, he drove to Tressa's antique shop in Rosemont.

He'd already been told Ron spent time in Rosemont at Tressa's apartment or at her shop with her, but since he'd gotten the Great Dane, he was at Verde most of the time. Through Thalia, again, he got a message to Ron, asking him to be at the antique shop this morning.

Marvin parked at the rear of her store, where there was a small loading area and a wide rear door with an unusual clear window at its upper half.

Emma Anders was just leaving through that door as he got out of his car. He knew Emma had clients whose financial records she kept up-to-date, and that Tressa was one of those. He also knew people were talking about three long rows of zinnias Emma and Reegie had grown. If you wanted to, you could buy a dozen zinnias you would cut all by yourself (Emma provided scissors) for three dollars, or you could have six for a dollar and a half.

"It helps pay for the chicken feed," was what Emma laughingly told people. To those not near the river, those zinnias caused some comment, because Cal and his brothers were pumping river water onto their farms and onto Shaggy and Emma's. It helped the soybeans… and the zinnias. Some farmers, more inland and not close to the river, were jealous of all that river water being used for irrigation.

Now, Marvin asked if he could stop by on his way home to get a dozen flowers, and he talked briefly with Emma before she drove away. Then he entered the shade and coolness of the back section of Tressa's world.

First, there was that little area with its desk and air conditioning duct, its shelves, where Emma worked, but beyond that, sort of around a corner from it, he could see Ron was sitting on a long bench behind some sort of shelving upon which was a cash register; below, shelves. This was where Tressa paid for some of the antiques coming in, where they would be repaired or re-upholstered and, when ready, then sent to the display room at the front of the store. There, other cash registers took money in for the things going out. Indeed, beyond Ron, Marvin could see Tressa was working on something, because that's what this whole back area was: it was a workroom.

Ron was looking down, twirling nervously some sort of silver-topped walking stick or cane. Marvin could see Ron's nervousness, and he figured Ron had seen him talking with Emma. He wondered if Tressa even knew that he, Marvin, had talked with Geraldine and Ron and that he knew already most of what he needed. Most, but not all.

Now, as he entered, he greeted Ron, "Guess you knew I would be coming here, didn't you, Ron?" And, when Tressa, surprised, turned from her work to look at him, he added, "I hope it's all right if I sit here next to Ron to ask some questions, Tressa."

He sat down next to Ron on the bench without waiting for an answer, and he took off his wide-brimmed straw hat. Ron's eyes got bigger when the hat came off.

"Guess that all depends on what questions you've got to ask," Tressa said.

"I don't have many. Geraldine has already told me most of what happened that ended with that hooker's death."

"Then, this evening Geraldine is getting fired."

"Everything she said, by the way, Ron here backs her up."

Now, she visibly twitched as she shifted her gaze to Ron. Ron seemed to cave inwardly.

"You don't have to worry. I'm not here to press any charges. But you've suffered a loss, Tressa, something you don't seem to know about. And there could be some other kind of trouble. I'm here officially to get around to it. Just let me get this done."

He turned his attention to Ron. "She'd been at your place more than once, kept yelling she was invited by you, was a guest, you owned the place... guess you told her that. Tressa, she thought, had no right telling her she must leave. Drunk and offensive, right?"

"Yeah."

"You were in your mother's bedroom, you had sex with her, and then maybe you went into the bathroom, and she was getting dressed. You came out of the bathroom and she was maybe standing at the chest of drawers where the jewelry box was, and she was partly dressed. You probably told her to get away from there. But when she moved away, the jewelry box was closed, right? And that's about when your mom came into the room and all hell broke loose?"

45

"Don't you tell him anything, Ron," Tressa said.

"Ron, we can do this here privately, or at the station where it'll be recorded. I know you don't want to talk about this part from the other day, but there aren't any charges... I'm telling you that, but there were those bruises on her, so we do have to... I need to get to something important here. So help me, please."

Ron hesitated, but then he said, "Right, and I was just trying to help get her out the back door and out of the house, but she kept kicking me in the legs and hitting Mom."

"Geraldine says she woke up and was watching out her window. She says you were sitting on the landing steps rubbing your legs, and it was Tressa who was having the big problem getting the girl into your convertible. Big fight outside, right?"

"Kind of. The convertible was closest, and the keys were in it. It's not Mom's fault she wouldn't go without a fight. Mom didn't get her drunk. She did that to herself."

"Right. If only there weren't marks on her from all that fighting. So, Tressa, you were taking her to the truck stop?" Now Marvin spoke directly to Tressa. "How'd she end up on the side of the road there?"

"I didn't push her out. When I slowed down to drive into the truck stop, she stood up on the back seat, and when I made the turn, she fell out, right into that ditch! I stopped in the parking lot, until I could see she was crawling out, and I just left her there. I headed back to the house. I could see when I passed she was sitting up in the weeds by the side of the road. I parked Ron's convertible where it was before at the house, got in my own car, and I went to Rosemont. I was so disgusted with Ron, I didn't want to stay. So neither Ron nor I killed her. Questions over."

"Almost, not quite. Just a couple more things." Now Marvin turned to Ron.

"See, there's something you two don't know. Because she'd been there before, I'm guessing, she'd spotted the jewelry box, and I think while you were in the bathroom, she already had it open and took something out of it. And then she closed it. I've had to figure out how I think things went, because the box must have been closed or you two would have known she took something. I've had to mull on this over and over. You almost caught her in the act of stealing something, Ron. She put it into her jacket pocket, and it was still there when her body arrived for autopsy."

"What did she take?" Tressa asked, aghast.

"It's a very expensive necklace. I've already spoken with the jeweler who sold it to you."

"Well, where is it, then? I want it back. Give it back to me."

"Be patient, Tressa, please!"

Again, he turned to Ron. "It's a good thing you gave me her name. I was able to find her parents, so she's had a funeral. But now here's the question I don't like asking. But I have to. Did she lead you to believe she was an adult, somebody older, maybe?"

"Well, yeah, sure. She had I.D. when we were drinking. Looked young, but—"

"She had fake I.D. Her parents told me she was close to seventeen years old. Her seventeenth birthday would have been some time later this summer. She was sixteen, a minor."

There was a silence that held for a moment.

Ron whispered, "She was a baby."

"I've been to her funeral," Marvin said. "The autopsy report and the funeral... both say the same thing: accident. Her parents still can't believe their daughter was making her runaway self into a hooker and a thief. I don't expect any problem. They don't want any bad things said about her, bad publicity. But you never

47

know, because as my boss, Davis, has reminded me, bad things happen when some shrewd lawyer gets hold of people. If only those bruises weren't on her. But they were. Tressa, if those parents charge you and Ron with sexual exploitation of a minor, Ron could go to jail. You could, too."

"What's that got to do with my necklace? I want it back *now*."

"Well, sure you do. But it has to stay in the possession of the sheriff's office till we're absolutely sure there's no legal action on the part of the parents. Let's just keep quiet. But if they did make charges, we can't use that necklace as proof of a low, thieving character if we let it out of our control. So it could be months before you get it back, Tressa."

"You son of a bitch! You've got my necklace!"

"No, not me. It's being held by the Sheriff's office. Out of my hands completely."

Now Marvin stood up, put his hat back on, and he moved closer to her. "Now, you understand me. If Geraldine was gone, somebody who could testify you were only trying to get her into a car, not beating her up to make her have sex with your son... if I couldn't find Geraldine, or if I found her, and she wouldn't come testify in Ron's defense, it would be a catastrophe. If you fire Geraldine, I will make it personal, and I'll see you never get that necklace back, ever. If you fire Geraldine, it's gone... for good. I'll throw it into the river."

He was ready to leave. He touched Ron on his shoulder. "This will pass soon. We'll be back working on our cars again—"

"He doesn't need advice, you son-of-a bitchin' half-breed!"

Marvin abruptly sat down again, snapped his hat off. "Tressa, I had to go tell her parents. Her father... I tried telling him to look at her left hand first... couple of rings maybe he'd recognize. He must have ended up seeing her head anyway. Some eighteen-wheeler at the truck stop... I bet the driver didn't even know the tail end of his rig hit her in the head. She probably walked right into it. Her skull, left side... skull completely detached, was hanging down over her eyes like a porch roof... you could only see a little part of her right eye. Even cleaned up... horrifying. I'm trying to prevent you from losing everything, even your child. It's hard to tell a parent I don't know he has to go see a dead child. It would kill me to see Ron in court for something like this. You're making this so much harder— even though it's hard—waiting to be sure. It might be a year before you get that necklace back—"

"A year? A year!"

But now Marvin was up and out the door. Ron, watching through the window-topped door, saw his car leave the parking lot.

His mother was peering into the front display room, where Niles Nelson, an older retired gentleman, worked on a commission basis to earn extra money. She was wondering if he'd heard any of their conversation. But Niles and two prospective customers with him were at the farthest end of the shop and were far from hearing anything.

Now, she whispered to Ron, "Did Emma hear us?"

"No." He assured her Emma left just as Marvin arrived.

And then Ron Gesler made the mistake of trying to comfort his mother, telling her it was going to be all right, that it wasn't so bad as all that, now was it.

Niles and his two possible customers certainly heard, and were shaken by the retort Tressa roared at her son. "You moron! You gave them her damn name!"

49

When finally he got home, much later, Marvin took the zinnias out of the tin can full of water Emma had given him. He separated the twelve zinnias into two bunches. He put them into mason jars, with water. One he put on the kitchen window sill. Just below that window sill, he could see the top of his father's head where he was seated on the porch reading the Verde newspaper that got published every two weeks. "Home again, Pop," he said.

"Hmm, good enough, then," came an answer.

"I stopped at Emma's and bought some zinnias from her. She and Reegie sent some banana bread for us."

"Have that then with coffee, maybe, after we eat?" Frank loved sweets.

Marvin knew his dad had fixed some succotash and some kind of bread he called Indian bread, and some meat that smelled good. Now, he took the other six zinnias out to his mother's grave.

As he entered the house, he stopped as he often did, opening a certain closet to be sure his mom's winter coat was still hanging there. Every now and then, he needed to remember her presence. Her fingers smoothing his hair or his collar as he entered school. The pockets always with good things... violets... the smell of those... or a cookie or a candy or a tissue.

He fell asleep that evening asking God to be aware of Ron Gesler.

The next morning, a Saturday, he resumed the splitting of the fireplace wood.

Marvin did a lot of wood chopping for his dad. Frank had heat and air conditioning in his humble home, thanks to Marvin, but he preferred living mostly in one area centering on the big fireplace. The wood-burning fireplace was a favorite thing for him.

Marvin thought maybe this had something to do with being an Indian. Frank told him once about people who had built modern homes for some Indians, and the Indian families tore holes in the walls so they could all be together in one place, especially around a fireplace. Marvin pointed out they lost a lot of heat going up that chimney with a fireplace; Frank said maybe so, but they got a lot more warmth, smiling as he said it.

For Marvin, that meant he started splitting wood in spring, and by end of September he figured that was enough. By then, he had sheds with wood stacked to the ceilings or on platforms with canvas coverings that kept the wood fairly dry.

His mind often wandered as he worked.

He had reasons to love Verde other than a sweet childhood with lots of friends. Some people of Verde had taken in Frank Dorset's ancestors, hiding them, keeping them safe, so that they didn't have to go on the Trail of Tears to Oklahoma. Marvin knew the Geslers and the Dorsets had sheltered Cherokee Indian families. Probably other families had, too. His father's people had taken the Dorset last name as their own. Frank and Marvin had been given the first names of some sheltering persons who were in that way being honored.

He knew his father had an Indian name, though. It was *Boy Who Remembers His Horses.* That was a nice name, Marvin thought, even though Frank never had any horses. Marvin kind of wished he'd had an Indian name, an extra name, a romantic one, something better than Marvin. Verde was a town full of nicknames. Marvin bet there wasn't even one nickname for Marvin.

Certainly, as he split and chopped, he often thought of his mom.

Even though he'd been very young, he could remember all

the kindnesses of his mother, and the softness of her words. He had thought, as a child, about where he came from. He'd decided that just as he came from his parents, those parents came from others, and so on, back and back into time... until what? Eventually, his little mind ran out of people, and what then? And he could remember figuring out, sitting there in his little chair at his little desk with the sun on his folded hands, that when there were no people, the very first ones had to come from the rocks.

Yes, that was it. The very first ones had to come from the big rocks, and that was why some people were so mean and cruel. They were the ones who had all that coming from rocks still in them so strong. So everything had to have arrived here that way, one step at a time, he decided, with stuff left behind at every step, so that if some terrible trouble came to everybody at the end of the trail... well, then, you had to start it all over again, from rocks, like at the beginning. Which explained why Ron's mother was certainly different from his.

Now, as an adult, he knew with certainty that if all the levels of hardness were to be removed from Tressa, what would be left would be some small, frightened thing, shivering and hiding, clutching the need to be surrounded by collectibles and antiques and things of value. The thing he would see before him would have come from poverty, and so it couldn't help being what it was.

When he had been driving away from Rosemont, he'd been thinking of Tressa, asking questions of her, mentally: *Did you give your new born children a kiss and whisper they were the best babies ever? Did you rock them, sing to them, tell stories? Did you decide that spot at the back of the baby's neck, where there was that one little curl of hair, was the best-smelling spot in the world?* Probably not, he'd decided.

Before he'd been able to have the attic ceiling fan and, later, air conditioning installed, there had been those restless summer nights when heat was stifling, when moonlight had made darkness retreat, when the whippoorwills were calling, and he'd been sleepless, punching his pillow. He'd faced then the fact he was thinking of Thalia, not so much just to defend or protect her, but to love her. He was in love with her. That made him suffer, for he felt helpless under the knowing of that. It just made things worse, and it made him almost hate Tressa, for Thalia seemed so alone.

After that stinging remark from his mother, Ron Gesler was glad to be home walking his dog. Driving back from Rosemont, he'd been troubled by one thing Marvin mentioned: only a small part of one of her eyes could be seen. Ron remembered her eyes.

Now, walking with Scrambler, he was relieved of that, living in the company of his dog. No matter what we've done, dogs seem to tell us we're not the bad guys. That was then, and this is now, and you're all right. That is what Scrambler meant, alongside him. His sister was taking up the slack, making sure there was money coming in, and he could, sooner or later, get a job. His mother would eventually calm down. She always did.

He took Scrambler on the side of the open grass lawn, far away from the garden shed, where, in the distance, he could see the seated figure of his father, hunched over his dreaded ax, probably drunk.

Now Hal chose to be, as usual, insulting. He called over the distance, "Well, now, aren't you a pretty sight! Who the hell said you could have that? Gonna leave turds all over the place big as an elephant's! Huh? Huh?"

Ron turned, answering across to his father, "Mom said it was all right."

He thought he heard something muttered back at him, perhaps about who owned this place, but he wasn't sure. His father turned away from him, and then there was silence.

Later, in his bed, in the darkness of the office, it didn't matter that he had neither a normal mother nor a good father. He had beside him this superior dog. Behind the locked door, he slept.

Hal Gesler wondered why in the world he'd ever married Tressa. He'd been adored by his grandmother, his parents, and his sisters. He was their shining hero, the only male child. He was an excellent student and athlete, and when he went to Chapel Hill, he'd been popular there. How in the world did all that go wrong? He'd been a happy fellow, right up till his marriage to Tressa.

Why would he pick for a wife someone who offered him insults and sarcasm every single day of their married life? His poor judgment bothered him every day now.

At Chapel Hill he'd had a steady girl. Holly was a tender, sweet person, but she wasn't submissive. When Tressa came into his life, he lost Holly almost at once, for as soon as Holly saw there was a sexual connection going on, she cut off all contact. He sometimes wondered what his life would have been like if he'd continued with Holly, if he'd married her. Probably it would have been normal, and he would have ended up happily married.

Certainly now he wasn't. Tressa had flowing good looks, and she had a most modern outlook about sex. In plainer words, with Tressa, the good times, sexually, began. She was the most exciting person he'd ever met, and she was also the first female to slap his ego down with insults. That was so novel and so unexpected, he just couldn't get enough of her.

When he married her, the insulting back and forth continued, and the more he gave to her financially, the more independent and insulting she became. Of course, he financed her antique shop in Rosemont, and yet the more successful she was, the less and less he got in return from her.

His family fortune began with his grandfather and father, both good businessmen. It began with the purchase of a large orchard of Stayman apples, so well suited for cooking and cider. Those apples stored well and could be released to market throughout the year. From that start, Geslers had been able to purchase farms for tenants to cultivate and homes to buy cheap and sell dear or rent out. There were acres of woodlands for lumber, some pine woods for pulp and for turpentine. There were even some purchases of local businesses and a few loans to businessmen that hadn't endeared Geslers to the banks.

At first, having a wife who wanted more and more of everything expensive didn't make a dent in the family finances, but eventually... well, the whole area was having a hard time now going on three years, and it stretched him thin. The drinking started even before children were born.

Having two children didn't make things any better. In a way, it made it worse. His own father had been a hard-working businessman, and Hal felt he had to keep up the business interests. It left not much time for anything else, and as the children grew, his anger grew apace.

He began to find pleasure with other women, thinking Tressa would care. She didn't. He hoped to find some satisfaction from the children, but that was disappointing, too. Ron was a slow student, handsome, but not brilliant, though he was a good athlete.

Hal felt Thalia hated him, and he couldn't blame her for that, for she looked so much like Tressa, he took things out on her, and at one point, he wanted her to give him the affection he didn't get from his wife. Whiskey gave him that faulty advice.

These days, Tressa showed up when she felt like it. He knew she had an apartment in Rosemont where she stayed most of the time. She came home to Verde now and then as if to check on the condition of her household possessions. And to smack him down a few times more.

Ron was no longer interested in him. Tressa always spoiled him, and Ron took his mother's side in everything.

Lou had disappeared, and it was a lonely life now. Hal sat where he felt he could still be recognized as the owner of this property. Yet, he felt the dislike for him so keenly, he never wanted to venture inside the house he boasted was his.

Sometimes he'd see Ron walking his huge dog on the other side of the open lawn that spread around the shed on two sides. Lately, he noticed Ron carried some plastic bags for picking up after the dog. Nonetheless, it irritated Hal, for it was as if Ron was going out of his way to ignore his father. There wasn't any need to be strutting around with a big dog and a fancy cane, as though Ron was the lord of some castle. It set Hal's teeth on edge to see his son pass him by and not even speak to him. From a distance, he admired his son, even though he was ever ready to criticize him. Ron's shoulders were, in fact, as broad as his father's, but he was so much more comfortably handsome than Hal was—with a dimpled smile and soft curls of hair—the things that softened women's hearts—Hal knew all that. But he never spoke of it. Hal had never given any sort of compliment to his son, nothing to make Ron know he had a father who loved him. It seemed more appropriate to criticize, as if that were a masculine way of showing caring.

Maybe the hot weather was making things worse.

Sometimes Hal wanted some ice water or some tea or something from his kitchen, but he didn't want to go into the house to ask Geraldine for it.

Without any explanation, Lou had disappeared, and he wondered why. Now and then, lately, the sky would grow dark in the west, as if a storm were brewing, and there would be a growl or two of distant thunder, but still no rain.

Now, this morning, when he came to his usual bench, his usual place, he saw there was a new wicker chair added next to the bench. There was a low small table, too. And inside the shed, Lou was there, putting some bags of rose fertilizer onto a wheeled dolly, preparing to take the load out to the rose garden. Off to the far right of the shed, on the west edge of the property, there were about thirty rose bushes close to the river that had been neglected during Lou's absence.

"Hello," Lou greeted him. "Guess I didn't get to let you know I had to leave, but I'm back now."

"Where the hell did you go?" Hal was pathetically glad to see Lou's partially bald head, and his long nose—those very things he'd once ridiculed (for his own head was still rich with hair, his profile admired), and now he felt a surge of gratitude that Lou had not, after all, left for good.

"New Jersey. My mother's folks. An aunt was ailing, and everybody's working, so I volunteered to help. She's better now. I hope you don't mind the chair and the table. Geraldine's got some lemonade, and I'll go later on and get that and a couple of sandwiches. If you want something to eat, join me. I'll need it, because I have to work on the roses. No rain hasn't helped them any. I have to get to them before it's too late."

Lou lied enthusiastically. He had no family in New Jersey. He settled into the wicker chair next to Hal to talk for a moment.

"Hard times with no rain. It'll take some work out there. Everything is suffering, I guess. Emma and Thalia working on the business today?"

"What's left of it. Not much they can do."

"Well, you just take it easy here, and when I get done, we'll at least have a cool drink. Might get rain later on, can't tell yet."

Hal couldn't know Lou had awakened before dawn from his sleep on the cot in the dining room (for Geraldine still wasn't letting him sleep in her comfortable bed with her). For a while Lou had thought about doing what he'd done the night before; he'd taken the blanket with him from the cot and sneaked into Tressa's bedroom. There, he had lain on top of the covers on her bed, wrapping the blanket around himself, and he'd slept comfortably. He wasn't afraid of getting caught in the royal bedroom, for he always woke up before anyone else.

But last night, instead, he had gone silently limping up and down the dimly lit first-floor hallway, thinking. Across from the office, Thalia was sleeping; Ron was with his dog in the front office, and Geraldine was in the back. Neither the owner of the property nor his wife was sleeping in the house. Neither the front door nor the back door was locked; in fact, Lou didn't even know if there were keys for those doors, or, if there were, where they might be.

That was when he decided that to help, he'd have to do more than just hide out from the old man. He'd have to befriend him, cultivate him, and tell Marvin if Hal got to be dangerous. He'd have to be able to observe Hal. And he resolved to get some locks and keys for the doors, too. Next morning, he told Geraldine what he planned to do.

Marvin had told him to be observant, to be in the house at night. Nothing else, much. But now Lou felt the need to do more.

"You took off because you can't stand the man, remember?" Geraldine said.

"That's true," he agreed with her. "But I need to be close to him to size him up, see what he's thinking. I want you to do me a favor. Has to be some shop in town where you can get some kind of big-headed cane. He's leaning forward, and he's puttin' both hands on top of that ax head or that ax handle, depending on which way he's got it, to put his weight, so he can see back of the house. He's looking to see if Tressa is here, if her car is here. That's what I'm thinking. If I give him a cane, if he uses it, I can slip that ax back away. And, listen now, I'm going to get locks for the front and back. And please have some drinks so I can keep him happy—maybe sandwiches, too. Maybe Miss Sterling's antique shop has some old canes."

She was looking at him thoughtfully. "You're starting to sound like Marvin," she said.

For a minute, Lou returned that long look. "You know something?" he finally said to her, "I think that's a pretty nice thing to say to me."

Joe Anders was an old-fashioned kind of farmer. Perhaps that was part of why he got along so well with Frank Dorset, another man who was set in his ways. He was a lot like Frank Dorset; his hair and eyes were as dark as any Indian's, as if his French mother's dark good looks had turned threatening in him. However, he wasn't a criminal sort; he was only centered on his family—and on his farm. And like Frank, Joe hated using too many chemicals on his crops. Instead, he relied on crop rotation—sometimes corn here, melons in another field, some fields sitting fallow, some being enriched by clover that he would plow under. He liked growing corn. People in these parts ate horse corn when it was young, and there were Amish and Mennonites nearby that always used it for their horses when it matured. It was an unfailing crop every time, along with melons, for everyone wanted those. Joe had seen Frank growing those crops, and he'd imitated Frank.

This year, Joe's big cash crop was to be soybeans. That was, if the drought didn't ruin the crop. Spring started off promising, but then it became dry.

He'd added to his knowledge about farming by seeking Frank out, questioning him. He'd seen how cleverly Frank would put in a cover crop, sometimes millet, sometimes sorghum, after his cash crop was harvested. He'd asked Frank about the way he planted clover and then plowed it under. "Why do you do that sometimes?"

"It seems to me it helps the soil and cuts down on weeds," Frank told him. There were many more topics they covered as they sat together under Frank's big old walnut tree, talking. He liked the way Frank rotated his crops; he did much the same thing.

He'd learned from watching the Petersons, too. He'd invested a few months ago in a huge, wheeled irrigation rig that allowed him to pump from the river. His was much like the rig the Petersons had. It needed a lot of power to spray great jets of water over the crops. It was expensive, and it had to be moved from place to place. It took a lot of strength to get it from one field position to another. This was a year when it was proving to be worth the effort. So far, irrigation was saving the day for his soybeans.

Shaggy made fun of Joe because he sometimes used a couple of old outhouses as bathrooms. When he needed to, he would stop his tractor or reaper and take a brief time-out to go sit in one or the other of the two he had placed alongside the fields. First of all, they were far distances away from each other, near different fields, but both of them looked out of place just the same, for they were nowhere near a house. When he defended his "poop stops" (that was what Shaggy called them), saying he read in Japan they fertilized the fields with human crap, everybody near him made faces.

However, since he was serious about the need for them, Reegie and Shaggy made an effort to be sure there was toilet paper in them, and he used lime in the outhouses every year to make sure they were as sanitary as they could be.

He also preferred water from the old artesian well not too far from the house. He said it tasted better than the spring water that arrived in big bottles Shaggy ordered from a company in Rosemont.

At one time, a bucket brought up water from the well, and everyone drank from the same old tin cup, but these days, Reegie and Shaggy would pour water from it into clean buckets and bring that into the house for him. From the buckets, the water went into pitchers with ice. It was a lot of trouble, but it pleased him. It was something like the grape arbors he kept for Concord grapes; it was easier to go buy some grape preserves, but the store-bought stuff was not as nice as what you cooked up for yourself from your own vines. Everything that came from your own hands, your own labor, was to be preferred.

He wasn't about to plant cotton, for that was too hard on the land, and he hated tobacco. Tobacco meant drying sheds, which he didn't have and didn't want to have.

His frugality extended to Shaggy's Great Dane bitch, a huge purebred creature named Skittles. She recently had puppies. In hard times, it was difficult enough to give away ordinary dogs, much less get rid of costly dogs that were going to be big and eat

61

a lot every day. Not only that, but inside the house was no place for a dog. If you had a herding dog, inside the barn was a good place for it. If it was a guard dog, why, the porch was where it stayed, except for cold weather when you let it in. Yet Shaggy insisted that this harlequin dog, so splattered with dots of black on white, was to be a house dog.

And why? Because the dog *spoke* to Shaggy, that was why. As far as Joe was concerned there were a great many improbable things that *spoke* to Shaggy.

"Daffodils speak to you," he said accusingly to her. "And none of them say anything sensible."

Thank goodness all the puppies were gone except for one. That one, a bitch like its mother, had a tawny body and darker face and ears like the typical Great Dane. Joe called her House Dog, because that was what she was, dammit.

"Dammit, Shaggy, I bet these two eat seven or eight cans of dog food apiece every day, at least." To his horror, he discovered it wasn't canned food at all. Rather, it was bags of dry food these giants ate, and when he looked at what was inside those big plastic bags, he found it was such roasted things as venison and buffalo.

"That's better'n what *we* eat," he protested. "If we get in a much worse way, we'll be barbequing those Great Danes of yours."

Inwardly he added, *I wish storm clouds talked to you.* He smiled to himself. He knew Emma, his sister, who came often to help out, and Regina, his mother—as well as Shaggy—had personal relations with everything on this farm. If they said a setting hen talked to them when they gathered eggs, no harm done. If it pleased those girls, pretend it made sense. And it seemed to him everything responded to the women.

One thing making Joe cranky was the threat of real poverty. They were getting along on the savings they'd managed to accumulate during the years before the drought when they had money to spare and put away, on insurance money from their father's accidental death, and on what Emma made from her CPA work in Rosemont and Steeds. A lot depended on those big irrigation sprayers pumping river water over his soybeans.

It made him even more frustrated that he was sick and getting sicker and didn't know why. For a while doctors thought he was being poisoned by somebody, and he thought they were looking at Shaggy funny. Finally they discarded that theory. Sometimes he was so strict about not spending money, he guessed folks thought Shaggy had a reason or two to want to get rid of him.

He spent a lot of time, when he absolutely had to, in a wheelchair. He was so tired sometimes he could hardly speak. If he'd paid attention to it, he would have noticed that House Dog had taken to being at his side. When he was thinking he wanted something, water or tissues or something to eat, the dog would go into the kitchen and, shortly after, following her, somebody or other would come along to see what was the matter and what would satisfy his need.

It wasn't until House Dog brought her empty water bowl to the side of his wheelchair and dropped it there with a loud clang that Shaggy noticed a choice had been made. "Looks like you've got a girlfriend," she told Joe.

"If she doesn't come with rich parents, I don't want her," he had managed to say hoarsely. But later, even he noticed the gentle dog was spending all her attention and time next to him, going to get people when he needed someone.

He owed a debt of thanks to Cal Peterson and his brothers,

Wes and Gunnar, for they had been coming and moving the irrigation rig around when needed. He made a mental vow to do something for them someday. When—if—he got well. He had begun to think it might be *if* instead of *when*.

It was nice to sit on the front porch in the morning. There he could watch the three dogs, Emma's and Shaggy's, play together. They acted as if they hadn't seen each other in years, tearing around joyfully. They were such different looking dogs, one all speckled, one so dark, one tawny, playing as if they were children.

Then came the afternoon he was sitting in his wheelchair, feeling lousy, on the covered patio on the east, where it was a little cooler with the sun beating down on the other side of the house. Shaggy and Emma had been shelling beans, sitting with him, and the three dogs were leaping around in the soybeans, which, on this side of the house, were growing closer to it.

Two of the dogs were, that is. House Dog was not. She was standing still, looking at him and Shaggy. "What the heck is wrong with that dog?" he said out loud, and Shaggy looked up from her work.

There was a little rut, or ditch, several inches deep, where the water from the irrigation rig had collected. The rut was at the edge of the little back yard, a line that divided yard from field. In the distance, Joe could see the irrigation rig throwing water on beans a farther distance off, and this water, from an earlier watering, hadn't soaked into the ground or dried up yet. The other dogs had sped over it into the soybeans, but House Dog was standing there like a statue, looking, it seemed to Joe, at either him or Shaggy. Now and then, it would bend its head down toward the water collected there. Occasionally, it was shaking its head and lifting one paw as it stood there, straddling the water.

Shaggy gasped. "Joe," she said, "I know what's wrong with you. House Dog just showed it to me."

The dog leapt off, joining the others in play. Later, Shaggy would tell Joe that when she met the gaze of House Dog, she saw, in her mind's eye, the bucket in the well, drawing up water. But the well water was being invaded by something very dark and sinister, and she knew at once it was water from the river, seeping into Joe's well. That water, so contaminated, must have had something about it the dog could sense, even though human beings could not.

Of course, Joe would make fun of her, but Shaggy would insist on it, and the spring water from Rosemont, as it arrived, would be what they would give to him to drink.

In spite of his protests, he began feeling better, and Reegie and Shaggy convinced him he should be drinking the same water they were. They told him they would start in again with the well water some day when the water levels were back up, but they covered up the well and nailed it shut.

It would take months for Joe to recover completely, and almost a year for his voice to sound as it once had. He quit making fun of the dogs. He did some reading about how dogs could detect things, even cancer.

"See?" Shaggy teased him.

In the days of recovery, he felt lucky. Even though it had been the river water that caused him to get sick, he knew how blessed he was, how he and the Peterson fellows had the river so close and were irrigating with sprayers. Most of the farmers he knew weren't located anywhere near the river and had no irrigation to save crops and keep them going.

In particular, he thought of his friend Frank Dorset. He knew what was on Frank's mind, that Frank was thinking pretty soon he would have to rev up his tractor and plow under the dried crops that died, how he would hope winter wheat could succeed where his other little crops failed. Frank would hope his orchard would give enough apples to have a little profit. It made Joe feel guilty. Here were hard times, and he was coming out of it better than most. It didn't seem fair.

One thing he had learned, and he thought this as he looked at House Dog, always near him—he now knew what dogs were really about; they were really about teaching us how to be observant.

Geraldine wasn't being very nice, much to Lou's surprise.

"It's not right, you spending all that time with him every day. You want back in my bed with me, you have to stop all that. Or at least, a lot less of it. I don't know why you're doing that, anyway. It's not going to do any good."

Lou was amazed. She hadn't said anything up to that moment about letting him back into her bed.

"It is helping. It's making him more... human."

So far, as he sat with Hal day after day, their time together was making Hal just that, a more settled person. He liked the cane Lou gave him with its heavy knob of wood for its head. The conversation at first centered on Hal's family; then it concentrated on his father and the start of the family fortune, and on how hard it was on Hal after his father's death to keep it going.

Lou had been a sympathetic ear and voice all along, and that helped Hal, but it also helped Lou. It helped both men when Lou talked about how his brother and he missed having a father in their lives. Lou well remembered the father who abandoned him, his brother, and their mother.

One day they saw Ron walking his dog along the edge of the

lawn's far side, about as far as Ron could get away from the gardening shed. To Lou's great astonishment, Hal stood up and called to Ron loudly enough for Ron to hear him, "What's his name, the name of your big dog? What's his name?"

Ron was clearly startled, as if he, also, was surprised. The big dog, stopped by his side, looked in their direction, wagging his tail, showing his friendly nature.

At first, Lou thought maybe Ron wasn't going to answer, but then the pride a fellow feels about his dog took over, and a joyful tone could be heard in his voice when he obliged with an answer. "It's Scrambler!" he called back. "He's called Scrambler!"

"Good! Good name!" Hal yelled across to Ron. When he sat down, he was smiling. It was the first time Lou had ever seen him smile.

Geraldine hadn't included a sandwich for Hal, so Lou turned his attention to cutting the one sandwich into fourths. He wanted to share it with Hal.

"If I had a father like you, I bet..." he continued talking, "I s'pose we could have gone camping or fishing. Maybe we would have gone to some ball games. I always wanted to have children, especially a girl. Geraldine probably would dress her up fancy, but I would have been all for keepin' her safe, protect her, you know, make her feel she would always have a home, no matter what..."

Now, when he glanced in Hal's direction, he could see that though Hal's hand was still clutching the big knobby head of his cane, and though he was seated, his head was almost bowed to his knees. His shoulders were shaking.

Hal Gesler was crying.

"He's been lonely, I think," Lou told Geraldine later. "Really, I think so. He's not going to hurt anybody, not anymore."

Geraldine was dubious, but Lou was back in her bedroom, to his amazement.

"I think Ron looks like you must have looked, when you were young," Lou had said to Hal.

"Do you really think so?"

"Oh, my, yes, and he's a very handsome young man." And for the second time, Hal smiled.

The two men didn't notice the little turtle headed toward the house, going in the opposite direction from them as they hurried toward the river. Lou had put a pump at the riverside with a length of garden hose extending from the pump into the river. The rest of that hose, so generously patched together, led to the rose garden Hal's grandmother had started so many years ago. Lou even made it a three-hose deal at its ending, spliced together with tape and glue, so he would supply water to the three rows of bushes at the same time.

"It'll work, you'll see," he said to Hal, who was skeptical about it. "The bushes are doing much better, and we just have to see they get water. I can't keep totin' it to them. Some of them have to go, but most are just fine."

Lou had electrical cord, lengths and lengths of it connected together, running from the pump to the inside of the garden shed. The two of them, working together, had run the electrical cords alongside the wooded side of the property leading out to the roses. "Well, now, let's see if this rig works," Lou said confidently.

"Probably going to cost a fortune in electric bills," Hal said, frowning.

"Nah, I don't think so," Lou countered. "I'll run it just every other day, in the morning only. I'll water one end first, early, and then, mid-morning, move it to the center of the rows, and then, when we're having some lunch, move it to the ends of the rows." He turned the pump on.

It worked. A small stream of water came from all three hose endings, pouring the needed water into all three rows.

The men rejoiced. "There'll be more than just a few roses," Lou predicted. "I can give Geraldine some. She's always wanting flowers for the front hallway, and you can give roses to Tressa and Thalia, and they'll be surprised!"

At the shed, they shared some egg salad sandwiches Lou had made for them. Geraldine had no part in it. Lou boiled the eggs the night before and then got up early to make the egg salad and the sandwiches. The tea he brought out to the shed was warm now, but it didn't matter.

"Well, we got that done, and pretty fast, too. This yard is goin' to look nice in no time." The two were happily grinning and eating. There wasn't need for a lot of conversation. The two men had become friends. They were planning on marigolds all along the perimeter of the roses. That helped stop bugs, they had been told.

Marvin was at one of his favorite places in town—the library. He was proud of the water treatment plant (it was a bragging point, how good their water was), the police department, where he spent so much of his time; and the diner, where he knew just about everybody who worked or ate there.

But the library was his favorite place because of Mary Williams, the librarian, who went out of her way to do extra things. In the children's section, she always had imaginative displays that drew children in, and in quiet corners she placed comfortable armchairs she'd slip-covered so folks could sit and read awhile. There were three computers, and if you had some things to look up, she would help you understand the ways of the Internet. Marvin was on one of those computers.

When through a side window he saw Thalia approaching the library entrance, he took off his easily recognized hat and closed Indian Affairs, switching over to Agricultural News, in case she saw him.

Sure enough, presently she tapped him on his shoulder. "What're you doin', Marvin?" she asked.

"Just looking up stuff. Why are you here?"

"Mary pulled some maps for me."

He knew about the German company that might be buying land, of course. It wasn't a secret. "I'd like to talk to you," he said. "How's about I treat you at the diner? I'll buy lunch." He was pleased when she agreed. His heart did a little hooray hip-hop as they walked to the nearby diner.

At first, after they ordered, the talk was casual. Mostly about the dog now named Scrambler, who had been taken over by Ron, and how much bigger that dog was now. But Marvin had a personal interest in the German company, and he spoke to that almost at once.

"You don't need those maps, Thalia. I've heard what they want, and so has just about everybody close to town. We've all heard some of the Petersons' farms, Joe and Shaggy's, Emma's, and my place and Dad's. We're all centrally located. We're in the middle of it all, whatever's being considered. I've heard rumors about what they want. I can tell you way ahead of time, Dad's not willing to sell. Neither am I. Maybe none of the rest, either. So I hope your German company is willing to build away from our farms, closer to Rosemont. Think so? It's just their plant, so it shouldn't be a problem."

Everyone eating, those in quiet conversation or studying the menu or a newspaper, showed no interest. Marvin's voice, as usual, was the quietest one of all, but the famers in the diner knew of the proposed German plant, and they were, indeed, listening. Where that plant might get located was of interest to them. It got quieter in the diner as soon as Marvin mentioned the plant. The diner hadn't been a cheerful place for many months. Those listening were quiet because they were skeptical.

"Well, I thought perhaps you could convince your dad to sell, that you could do that for me," Thalia said.

"My mother's grave is on that property," Marvin said softly. "He won't be convinced—not by anybody."

For a moment she was silent, hesitating, but then she decided to go ahead. "Her remains could be moved to some other location," she said with some conviction, as if that would be an easy thing.

Now eyes were appearing from under the hats, and chairs were silently being turned toward the table where Marvin and she were, where Marvin sat and now she stood.

"Thalia—" he began, but she interrupted.

"It's gotten to be a bigger deal, anyway." She was happy, it was clear to everyone, about this "bigger deal," whatever it could be.

"What?" Marvin asked.

"Well, Norfunt is the name of the company, and now they've got an American Realty company that's going to be working with them. That company's called FloEast, and they want to buy up all the land they can in this region. All of it, and I guess they figure nobody's making more land—"

"What?" Marvin tried again, softly.

"Well, now Marvin, they'll have a development here, and

what isn't developed right away will get developed eventually."

"What you're saying is that farms will disappear, farmers will disappear, as if a bomb went off."

"Marvin, for God's sake. It's a good thing, actually. They're offering $55,000 an acre."

It was as if an electric shock went through the diner. Some were figuring in their heads; some actually had stubby pencils or pens figuring on the paper napkins next to their plates their acreage times 55.

"It's as if you're using money as a weapon," Marvin said accusingly.

"No, I'm not!"

"Well, how do you know there's any other place where so many farmers could go to farm, starting all over again, anyway?"

"Maybe it would be better if they *didn't* farm anymore," she said briskly.

Now Marvin stood up, and he put on his worn hat. He stood taller than she. "Kind of making their decisions for them, don't you think?"

"I'm doing no such thing. It's this drought that's making the decisions for farmers around here," she exploded. The dark eyes of the man who wasn't brave enough to commit to any woman met head on with the blue eyes of the woman who was afraid to commit to any man, and love stumbled.

"It's like you're cutting a hole in some old quilt, and then you're going to fix it with the wrong kind of material, wrong color," he tried to explain to her.

"They're going to want some assurances the people in the area are comfortable with the idea of this development," she said quietly, cooling down, "or they won't come to close any deal. I guess you'll do everything you can to stop it."

She closed up her zippered case of papers, which Marvin later guessed she had wanted to show him, and she left.

Now he sat down. The waitress, Wanda, brought what they'd ordered, and she wanted to know if she should take Thalia's order back. Yes, but he'd pay for it. He ate a few bites of his own lunch, and then concentrated on coffee, which always made him think better.

He was going to have to talk with his father. Every person in the diner would be talking with someone this evening.

Jess Wilson stopped on his way out and patted Marvin on the shoulder. "I guess I'll just be out of a job, then," he said. He was a tenant farmer. "See you later, Marv." If Marvin had been thinking, he might have marveled that at last someone had made a nickname out of "Marvin." He was cross with himself. He hadn't acted like a friend. Thalia probably wouldn't speak to him ever again, he told himself.

Frank Dorset sat on the bench where he loved to sit, usually, under the walnut tree, but today there wasn't much pleasure in it. When you're older, sometimes parts of your body rebel when you get tired, and today it was that right leg of his that was trembling after he'd spent so much time and effort plowing his tomatoes under. He had started his tomatoes late this year, and at first they did well, but the drought finally caught up with them, so today he'd done away with them. He'd left the onions, though. Like so many farmers, he planted companion crops: corn, growing high; and squash, growing low; and always onions along with wheat and the tomatoes. Usually he would supply the local roadside stands and local markets, and take tomatoes to the canning factory, but this year, it looked as if he'd have little to show. He hoped his apples would hang on and ripen.

73

Marvin had warned his dad, when he was telling about the German plant interested in moving to their farming area "This will l probably get unpleasant." Marvin had added, patting his dad's shoulder, "We'll have to stay strong."

Right now, Frank wasn't feeling very strong. He'd been busy on the tractor and hadn't heard noise, and so the work of vandals took him by surprise. He came in from the field to find someone had bashed his mail box. It was lying on the ground, caved in, with its pole sticking up all alone. And they'd destroyed his pickup's windshield. Then they'd thrown their long-handled hammer onto the house porch. It was lying near the front door. He was left to consider all this with his right leg jiggling around. He felt weak. This because, he knew, people already were eager to sell, and they figured he was in the way of that.

How, at this moment, he missed Ellie. It put him in mind of when he'd seen her for the first time. He was working the farm alone, for his mother had died the previous winter, and his father had passed on the fall before that. When he went into town, he always seemed to pass her family farm when she was there at the mailbox. They started waving at each other. Finally, one day, he stopped to introduce himself to her. Asked her once, years later, why she took an interest in him, and she told him she saw he needed her. That was typical of Ellie, to step in and fill a need.

When she up and moved in with him, and when she was pregnant with Marvin, her family wrote her off. It was especially repugnant to them she was pregnant when they got married. All Frank knew was there was never any doubt they would marry. Everything happened fast with them, that was all. He always felt faint from happiness when he was with her. For those years they were together, the three of them, he was supremely happy. Till Ellie got sick, of course. That happened fast, too, her death.

And now he was expected to be strong. He was sure he could pretend to be, but if it was to be not only the weather but also his neighbors who would pick on him, he wasn't sure he could be strong for long.

When Thalia called him, wanting to come out to talk to him, he knew what she would want to talk about, but he said yes. He knew he was still plenty strong enough to say no. He hadn't seen her in a long time, so that would be nice. When he told her no to the idea of selling out—maybe nobody ever said no to her—he would be kind about it. He was always strong enough to be kind.

Thalia had never been to Marvin and Frank Dorset's place. She'd heard a little about it from Laurie Jamison, who'd dated Marvin for a while. Laurie hadn't been impressed.

The first thing Thalia saw was the walnut tree her grandfather had tried to buy for its lumber. That had been years ago, and now the tree was huge. Frank was sitting on a bench under its shade. Maybe Laurie hadn't been impressed, but Thalia certainly was. At first she thought it was an oak, it was so tall, and its trunk so big.

The house behind Frank was a study in shades of rustic brown. It seemed larger than it probably was because there was a wide, covered, wrap-around porch on all sides. The porch was interrupted by worn steps with no supportive railing going up to it at the front. There was also, she could see on the porch, a stone chimney with fire wood stacked beside it. She had the feeling the house began smaller, but something had been added on one side (perhaps a bedroom or nursery?), and there were some windows and a smaller roof line appearing above the rear of the house, so something had been added there, too. For just a moment, she wondered if there had been plans for more than one child. She fought back the urge to ask to go inside, for she wanted to see if the fireplace was as large and as welcoming as it hinted it might be. It was undoubtedly a wood-burning, stone-faced fireplace.

Frank had set out a wooden folding chair for her so they could face each other and talk. There was a pitcher of lemonade on a low metal table between them, and there was a glass for her there. Frank was already drinking from his own glass. When she arrived, Frank poured some lemonade for her. He seemed glad to see her.

"You know why I'm here?" she asked.

He smiled and nodded yes. In a vase with water in it, she'd brought some red zinnias Emma insisted she carry. "These are for your wife's grave," she said.

He pointed, and she saw, a short distance away, under some shade trees, an area surrounded by a low, white picket fence. She could see the cross at its center. "I'll take these there a little later on." The flowers had water; they could wait.

"What was your wife's name?" She had heard some things— that she was a white woman, that she was the daughter of a good family, that the family disowned her after she moved in with Frank and got pregnant.

"Ellie. Her name was Ellen, but we called her Ellie. Her spirit is content resting here, so I can't move her. Marvin said you mentioned that."

"I did mention it. Because it might be she would like it fine if you were near other Indians. Do you think that might be?"

"Other Indians. Lots of spirits of other Indians still here. They were here first, before anybody else, you know. Then came the whites and liquor and gambling, and some Indians liked those things. The hunters of some villages liked them so much, those things, they didn't hunt as much as they drank, and when that happened, everybody suffered in winter because they hadn't hunted as much. And now it's money. That changes things, too. And drought, that too. But still, this is home, and I want to stay here."

She changed the subject. "I've heard about this walnut tree. I think my grandfather tried to buy it, didn't he?"

"Yes, he wanted her hard heart of wood. She's a tough old woman. The children she throws down, they have a hard shell around them, too. She's not for sale. Anyone can come pick up walnuts. You, too."

"I didn't hear a dog when I got here. I heard you have one."

"Once we did. We had some sheep, a few. But sheep crop the grass all the way to the ground and we didn't have enough grassland, so we gave them away, because we didn't have land that had grass enough, and the dog went with them, because he felt caring for the sheep was his life's work. He wanted to be with them. I hear you have a dog now, though. Something from Joe's house, a big guard dog, is it?"

"I'm not sure. He's so friendly, he might not scare off any robbers."

Frank smiled. "Well, maybe some dogs make it their business to teach us how to be friendly with where we are, what we are, you know. Friendly with the spirits of a place."

"There are places, surely there are, where they don't have droughts like this. Frank, there are better places for farming."

"Once, Indians believed there was a spirit living in just about everything. Maybe I'm like Joe's dogs, your dog, just wanting to stay put and be friends with a place and with the spirits of a place. I don't know what my girls, my daughters, would think if I wasn't here in November."

"Your girls? You have daughters?"

"There's the tallest trees, and they're for lumber, and those are males, men. But the fruit trees, the orchards, that give fruit, those are females. In November, at full moon every year, once it's dark, I go from tree to tree, and before they go into deep sleep, I wake them up for a little bit. I stop at each tree, put a branch into some wine, and I tell them, each one, to remember as they sleep, that in spring, I'll be there to meet them, take care of them. And while they sleep, I want them to know I'll watch over them. It's important. It's like putting your kids to bed. If I didn't do that, I guess the apples wouldn't be so good the next season."

Later, Thalia leaned over the low fencing to put the vase and the zinnias next to the cross where the wife's name was shown: Ellen Fitzgerald Dorset. "You have some stubborn men, Ellie," she whispered.

When she'd asked Frank what Ellie looked like, Frank said, "Like all things beautiful. She had blue eyes, kind of like yours. This time of year, she'd always be canning or making pickles, something. Wiping her hands on her apron, when she finished some project or other."

He looked over toward her grave. "'Well, good enough, then,' that's what she always said when she had finished some project or other. I say that myself, sometimes, because I remember her saying it so much."

It could be it would take a meeting to move things forward. Yes, if some school would let her use their auditorium, some school closest to town, and if she could get FloEast or Norfunt to send somebody to speak, to answer questions, then maybe if everyone was ready to sell, they could put pressure on the few holding out. That would be worth a try, surely. Thalia was thinking that.

As she got into her car, getting ready to leave, Marvin pulled up, coming home from work. When he got out of the car and stood, he noticed her. He tipped his hat to her, but he wasn't smiling. She noticed, of course, that Marvin was taller than any of the Peterson brothers, certainly taller than her brother, Ron, and he was a very handsome man, even as he looked so stern. The muscles of his cheeks were twitching.

Then she could see, clearly, that he was looking at the smashed windshield of his dad's pickup. Some people had chosen vandalism to try to convince Frank he must sell.

Emma's Journal Entry

*Cal came to help move the irrigation rig, but I think he came to start an argument, too. It started when he asked Joe if he would sell and if Reegie and I would sell, too.*

*I'm proud of my brother, Joe. He's not tall and handsome or as young as Cal. He's a lot shorter. I know Shaggy thinks he's handsome, but she would. What I like is how Joe is straightforward. So he said Hell no, we're not selling. Joe's voice is still not so good, and he sounds like some kind of monster. Cal said Then it's your bunch and old Indian Frank keeping everybody poor, and Joe said No, we aren't, and Frank was just plain Frank and not old Indian Frank. He's a friend, and if Cal and his brothers wanted to sell, nobody was stopping them.*

*Then Cal said Joe knew good and well just a few could ruin and stop everything. And Joe said If they want to buy you out, they'll buy without us along.*

*Cal couldn't shut up, and he said didn't Joe know how everywhere so many people were quitting farming and farm life? Joe said that was their business. And Cal said he was tired of farm life and all the worrying. Joe said it sounded to him more like Cal was tired of all the caring about anything.*

79

*House Dog had herself sort of between them, and her nose was right on Cal's hand, so Cal said Damn dog big as a horse and your dog better not bite me. Shaggy was behind Joe and she said She's not going to bite you. She's just trying to tell you to unclench your fist. Cal said How do you think you know that? And Shaggy said She told me, and then Cal said Shaggy was a crazy woman.*

*That made Joe mad, and he said Just how do you think millions is the answer to everything, anyway? You want to be on a beach somewhere, far off, don't know the language or anybody who lives there, or the lay of the land, just sitting there, nothing to do? Just sitting on your ass all day? If that's what you think is so hot, Shaggy's not the crazy one.*

*Cal left, but when he walked close to me, he slowed down and stopped and gave me a long look. Joe says now he's glad he's on his feet again, even if he can't talk so well yet, and guess Marvin can help him move the irrigation rig next time. Everyone knows there's going to be a meeting soon about all this and everybody knows ahead of time it's just us and Frank against it.*

*Joe says we're going to have a hard time because of this. He says to get ready for it.*

The windshield was replaced, but the dented driver's side door would have to be tolerated. Just one more thing that an old pickup had to mar its looks. Marvin was putting a new mailbox onto its post when Cal Peterson drove up.

He wanted to talk.

"Fine. But it won't do any good."

"Not about that. About something else."

"So not about the meeting coming up about the land sale?"

Marvin stopped what he was doing and led the way to the

walnut tree. They sat there, facing one another, Frank's pitiful little table between them.

"We sat here a lot, high school days, didn't we?" Cal began.

"Yep. We did."

"I wish we could go back to that, to being all friends again. I miss it a lot."

"Yep. Me, too."

Then Cal blushed, and Marvin noticed it. "What's really bothering you, Cal? Something on your mind?"

"You ever think about Emma, Marvin?"

That set Marvin back, because he certainly did indeed think of Emma, but not in any way that suggested to him she was a possible date. She was too daunting.

"Why would you ask that, Cal?" he finally ventured cautiously.

"Well, when we were in high school, she and Thalia were the best looking. I knew Ron had his eye on Emma, but he never did anything. So I wondered if you had an eye out for her, too."

"Ah—"

"Well, you know she hurt me when she told me about her and Ron. Guess you know that. Gives a fellow no choice, you know."

"Cal, I'm no preacher or anything, but you could have talked to Emma, maybe have forgiven her before you got the divorce."

"Too hard."

"Oh. Well, that's that, then."

"It's just that even when things are over with, you know, there's still that interest in the person you were married to—a concern for her, you know—not wanting her to get hurt, you know."

"Uh-huh."

"I mean, if Ron got together with her, it wouldn't be a good thing, would it?"

Marvin was silent.

"You think?" Cal persisted.

"What's made you think of all that, anyway?" Marvin asked.

"Well, I do hear he's settled down a lot, now he's got his dog,"

"So?"

"Well, there's a possible job for him. At the truck stop on Route 40, on the way to Rosemont, that one. A mechanic left there, so they need somebody. So I told that guy Andrew about Ron, and I gave Ron Andrew's name and phone number. I told him to call."

"What's wrong with that?"

"Well, what if he gets that job and then he gets close with Emma again, and I caused that to happen, and if she gets hurt— from him—then I caused that. See? So do you think I did the right thing?"

"A little late to be worrying, don't you think? Anyway, what you did was try to help him, and that's a good thing. Whatever happens, you didn't do a bad thing."

"You really think so?"

"Yep."

That evening, long after Cal had left, Frank and Marvin sat together in the kitchen, and he told his dad about that conversation. "Fellow is worried a little too late about Emma," Marvin said.

Frank was thoughtful. "Do you remember that dog we had for guarding the sheep?" he asked.

"Yes, sure."

"That dog got fed out of a big food bag, you remember, feed

82

mixed with water to make gravy. He never got a single thing out of our refrigerator. Not one piece of cold leftovers, not one piece of cheese, not one thing did that dog ever get out of that refrigerator. But every time he was let in the house, every single time he got in, he always had to stop and piss on that refrigerator. It was his way, the dog's way, of saying, 'This is mine. This refrigerator is mine. Yes, belongs to me,' that's what the dog was saying. Cal's like that dog, pissing on the refrigerator when he's not getting a damn thing out of it."

For a minute, both men were quiet. Then Frank added gently, "I always thought Cal was smarter than that."

Marvin didn't get on his knees when he said prayers. But he wanted prayer, especially tonight, when he was still fretting with himself about arguing with Thalia. Lying in bed, he said his piece with the Lord. He prayed his mom would be at rest, at peace; that God would end this awful drought; that he could have more years with his dad; that the poor prostitute girl who'd been killed would be in Heaven, no matter what; and that the sale of farms wouldn't happen. He prayed all of that. Then he added, and he couldn't help it—he did snicker—and please, Lord, stop Cal from pissing on the refrigerator. He wondered if Thalia was asleep.

Who knows how a turtle thinks? Why would a turtle leave a weedy, wet spot beside the river to travel past the rose garden, over a long expanse of lawn to get to the garden work shed, past that, to the corner at the front of the house? There the turtle rested overnight, and next morning it set off again. The ultimate goal was to get across more wide lawn space to the mailbox, then across the road, till at last it reached another weedy, wet area next to the river where that shallow waterway doubled back upon itself. Perhaps there were relatives the turtle wanted to visit. This appeared to be its travel plans.

This morning, Ron was in a rush. He was expected to be at the truck stop by a certain time to interview for a job, and he had overslept. He showered and shaved, and then he dressed, all in great haste. Scrambler watched him leave. Ron hurriedly shut the door to the office behind himself. He was careless. His mind was already thinking about proving himself to be a good auto mechanic.

The door in the hallway that opened to the outside world wasn't really closed tightly. Ron had shut it with much emphasis, so much so that it bounced back away from the door jam. It was closed, but not *really* closed. A good shove would open it. When Ron left from the front door of the house, it was loosely closed, but it would open when a little pressure was applied.

"You be a good boy till I get back," he had said to Scrambler.

For quite a long time, Scrambler was just that; he was a good dog, lying on the bed, nuzzling a stuffed toy. Ron was going to be away for a long time, for he was working on some cars that needed repairs, showing the man named Andrew that he could fix cars, just as people said he could.

Hours passed. Scrambler began trying to look out windows, to see if Ron was nearby. Then he pawed at the door and was surprised when it gave way and opened. The front door also gave way when this intelligent dog realized it was like the first door and could be opened.

Scrambler was then standing on the front steps of the house, looking about to see if Ron was around. Normally, the dog would have followed the route he and Ron so often followed, heading toward the back of the house, then skirting the far side of the lawn, across from the garden shed, to the river's edge and back.

If he had gone in that direction, Hal would have seen him and would have called him and kept him safe.

But that didn't happen. Scrambler had never seen a turtle, and now he caught the scent of one, and at about the same time he spotted the little turtle moving so slowly across the front lawn toward the mailbox and the road. He went to investigate it.

The turtle was as tolerant as it could be of a dog sniffing about, pawing at it, and then mouthing it between what the turtle must have seen as monstrous, big jaws. A couple of times it drew its head into its shell, and stopped for a bit, only to resume as soon as it thought it could begin again.

Elias Thomas was driving the bakery delivery truck, and he certainly wasn't speeding, for it was an old, heavy, loaded vehicle, and he wasn't in any hurry. When Scrambler tossed the turtle up in the air, Elias saw something dark, with short moving legs, land in the road ahead of him, and he saw at once it was a turtle.

Some people don't think far enough behind or far enough ahead. If he'd been thinking in either direction, he would have acted differently. But because he was barely out of his teens, and because he wasn't that considerate of a turtle's life, Elias decided at once he wanted to run over that turtle. He wanted to know he'd crushed its shell, snuffed out its life. He steered directly at it.

At the precise moment he would have killed the turtle, Scrambler appeared in front of the truck.

The large dog was directly in front of the truck, looking up at it just as it smashed into him. The dog's head was crushed against the truck's bumper and grillwork, and its body was tossed yards ahead of the truck. There was no time to hit the brakes until moments after it happened.

Elias stopped and emerged from the truck, and he could see

the dog, though still moving a little, was dead. If there had been anything he could have done to help, Elias would have done it, but it was hopeless.

He thought it looked as if it might be some expensive breed, so he pulled the dog away from the road, thinking its owner might find it with no more damage done to it by other cars or trucks. There was some blood on the road and a little on the dirt, but the animal had not much damage except to its head. Now Elias dragged its body past the mailbox he saw nearby, and up that lane a little way, leaving it there where it certainly would be seen.

Just before Elias pulled away in his truck, the turtle righted itself and now emerged from beneath it. The truck's wheels came close to crushing it, but somehow the turtle made it to the other side of the highway and went into the weeds. It was on its way to another weedy wet spot just like the one it left. It had no idea it had just come close to death.

Ron found his dog's body in the lane when he returned from a couple of hours working at repairing a car, getting a job. He had been jubilant as he arrived home, but now he was silent, stunned.

When Thalia drove into the lane, she discovered Ron cradling his dog's body. "Him and his damn ax," was what Ron said. "My God, look at what he did to him, and then he put him here so I would damn well find him." Both, after that, were wordless.

Ron laid Scrambler's body just under the office window. He entered the house with Thalia right behind him. He paused at the office door. "I never locked it. When I left, my father must have gone in here and... my *father* did this? What kind of father does..." He looked at Thalia, wide-eyed, dumbfounded.

"Right now I don't want you to be alone. I came to see if you'd have lunch, later... but now... Listen, now, Ron. You're my brother, and I love you. Go to the kitchen and talk with Geraldine. Tell her what's happened. I have to go back to the office because a call will be coming in at any moment or any time, maybe even an hour or so from now. Will you go there now? To the kitchen? I'll be back soon as I can. If you love me, please go." Thalia half expected he would ignore her, but he nodded yes and went down the hall toward the kitchen. She watched him go into the kitchen before she left.

Geraldine and Lou were arguing about marigold seedlings. Lou and Hal had quite a few flats of marigold plants started in the garden shed. Since there weren't any chickens or guinea hens they could let loose among the rose bushes to scratch up insects and eat them, the next best thing, according to Lou, was to plant marigolds. The two men wanted to plant them all the way around the rose bed, all along its perimeter on all sides.

When Geraldine asked why, Lou said it was because marigolds were supposed to repel insects.

Geraldine took issue. "That's a bunch of nonsense," she said. "Besides, you still spend way too much time with that man."

"We're just improving the rose garden. Besides, he's more settled and normal now." Lou turned and addressed Ron where he sat at the kitchen table. "You'll be impressed, Ron, how he's different now."

"Yes, I'll want to see that," Ron's answer came, softly.

Geraldine put a sandwich in front of Ron. "Leftover meatloaf," she said. "I know you like it. Right?"

Ron nodded yes.

"There's some pudding in the fridge, too. We're going to be out for a little while, since Lou's so set on getting that mulch right now."

"I'll probably have to help load it into the car," Lou added. "Come on, let's go get this done. We'll be right back, Ron."

He waited till he heard the car start, and he gave it plenty of time for them to be out the driveway and gone before he moved.

Hal wondered why Lou was so late today. He watered the marigold seedlings and fussed over them for a while, and then he sat in his wicker chair in front of the garden shed, waiting.

He'd become almost childlike in his expectations for the rose garden. He was looking forward to planting the marigolds around the borders of it. He felt sure they'd soon have great bunches of roses to show for their efforts. Why, he'd give roses and roses and roses to Thalia and apologize to her again and again and again, till she would forgive him. He was going to be such a better man, and no drinking, for he'd already stopped that and hanging out at bars. Perhaps even Tressa would begin to respect him.

He and Lou, they could go camping and fishing with Ron, and maybe even go to baseball games. There was a wonderful world of opportunities opening up.

There was a wind kicking up, flipping the leaves of trees over, so that he wondered if a storm might be coming, for sometimes a sudden wind change could signal a storm.

That was when he noticed Ron had come to the lawn across from the shed. He'd come from the back of the house, and now he was standing still over there, not looking at Hal at all, just smiling, casually flourishing his cane, looking off in the direction of the mountains.

Hal sat quietly, admiring his son. The wind ruffled Ron's curly hair and the collar of his shirt. What a handsome son, Hal couldn't help thinking, remembering all the soccer games, baseball games, football games—all the team sports in which his boy had played. He felt such pride, and he was about to call out to his son, but just then Ron began walking purposefully toward him.

He came wagging the cane playfully, as if he were one of many men, as if he were part of some military line that was facing artillery and didn't care, wasn't afraid. He was looking at his father now, and smiling broadly.

Hal Gesler stood up and went forward to meet him, his arms outstretched as if to give Ron a welcoming hug. There was a smile on his face.

There was still a smile on Hal's face when Ron slipped the blade out from the cane and ran his father through with it. Even after Hal was on the ground, Ron struck him again and again with it, till he saw blood from his father's open mouth, till he was sure his father was dying.

He left the shed and went into the house again. There he made a phone call to the police, asking the woman who answered to let Marvin know he, Ron, had just killed his father, and Hal's body was at the garden shed.

He drove off in his convertible.

Marvin had left his office, left the station, after he got that message, as if his hair were on fire. When he found Hal, Hal was not dead at all but was alive and conscious. At first, he tried to tell Marvin there'd been an accident.

"That won't work, Hal," Marvin told him. "How is it you think I'm here? Ron called and left a message. He thinks he's killed you."

"I don't want any charges pressed against my son,"

"I don't care about any charges. But I sure as hell want to find him, though. Right now, I have to leave you and see about getting some help here. Don't run off."

"Very funny."

When Lou and Geraldine came back, they found police and an emergency medical team had taken over, and when Thalia arrived, she added to the confusion. But when Lou and Geraldine were back in the house, and when police and the ambulance had left, Thalia and Marvin were standing there, alone. "I think perhaps you'd better call your mother," Marvin suggested.

"That won't work. She never answers the phone."

"Why not? It's a business number—"

She shrugged. "Some sort of thing about stolen property. It's always Niles or his wife or whoever else is there answers."

"Who knows what she's going to hear, then."

"So I'll leave now and drive there and tell her."

"Well, there is one other matter. I'll drive you there myself in the squad car. There is one thing could need to be done now. Could help."

"I can do this myself, thank you!"

"Listen, then! It's not necessary to drive two cars when one would do. I'm sorry we've argued, and I don't intend to argue again. If you insist, I can follow you down in my car. I just have to stop at the station to get something."

"Do that, then." She sped off. He was left standing speechless.


From the vantage point at her bedroom window, Geraldine reported to Lou.

"Well, they've argued. And off she went."

Lou shook his head regretfully. He'd heard what Thalia said to Marvin, about the dog's death, how Ron reacted, how she felt sure Hal had killed Scrambler with his ax, where the dog's body was.

He'd hastily gone to that place, just under the office window at the front of the house, and there was no dog's body there.

"He couldn't have done anything with his ax," he said to Geraldine. "He didn't even have that ax anymore."

Even though he'd stopped at the office, Marvin was able to catch up with Thalia as she drove to Rosemont. When she pulled into the parking lot and stood at the antique shop back door, he was right behind her.

Tressa opened that rear door for Thalia, and she didn't seem pleased that Marvin was with her. "Niles already got the news, and I've been told," she said at once. She wasn't shedding any tears, that was clear.

"Why the hell are *you* here, anyway?" she asked of Marvin.

"Don't suppose you've heard from Ron today?" Marvin replied.

Tressa settled into a wing-backed chair she'd been working on. "I wouldn't tell you, if I had." She was self-assured, comfortable.

Now Thalia asked, "What did Niles tell you, Mom?"

"He told me Ron killed Hal, that's what."

Thalia looked distressed. "Well, that's not true, not yet, anyway. Hal's still alive, in the hospital, and they're looking for Ron."

Tressa's facial expression changed at once. Now, she was enraged.

"Are you telling me that bastard is still *alive*? Is that what you're saying? And Ron is going to be arrested for trying to give that asshole what he's deserved for years? Is that why you're here?"

"Mom, please—" Thalia began.

Now, Tressa was on her feet, facing her daughter, closing in on her.

"You shut up, you two-bit nothing!"

Marvin moved in smoothly, easily, between Thalia and her mother.

"No charges are being made against Ron, Tressa. Hal's not having it. And Davis told me the parents aren't getting any lawyer, so he says there's no problem giving you back this necklace. I thought this would be a good time to give it to you." He pulled the necklace out of his shirt pocket and handed it to her.

She calmed down at once, taking it in hand and looking at it, examining it.

"We're leaving now, or at least I am. If you hear from Ron, please tell him he hasn't killed anybody, and he should relax."

As he turned to leave, a tearful Thalia was pressing close behind him.

Outside, he spoke softly to her. "Is it too much to ask, if just once you listen to me? I'm going home, and I'm going to have a drink. You should come, too, just to sit a minute, have a drink, breathe easy, get over this. But you do as you damn well please. I've had it today." He told himself he meant it, even as he reluctantly left her to drive away alone.

When he got home, he greeted his dad as usual. Then he went into the bathroom for a while, splashing some water on his face before he left. In the kitchen, he poured a double shot of whiskey over some ice cubes and added a little water. He headed for the front porch. Time now to relax and try to forget Thalia.

He was surprised to hear voices and to see Thalia was seated near his father beneath the walnut tree.

Frank had fixed a lemonade sort of drink spiked with vodka. And he and Thalia were talking together as if they were old buddies who'd had a drink or two before. He chose not to join them. In the first place, he was nervous about where Ron could be, what he knew. And what the hell? Wasn't she hating him, but here taking up his father's time? Borrowing his Pop away from him? Yeah, that's what, borrowing his Pop away from him.

Later, after she was gone, Marvin learned Thalia had been coming to sit under the walnut tree to talk with Frank from time to time for a couple of months now.

"Pops, don't you know she's trying to get us to sell and move out?"

"Well, yes, that's why she came the first time. But later, I think she comes because she needs somebody to talk to. She knows we're not moving, not selling."

"Oh yeah, and you're such a charmer, you're it, huh, the very best person to talk to."

"You know how women are. I look like some chief they saw in a Geronimo movie," Frank laughed. "She says you sort of saved her, talking to her mother. Do you think Ron will turn up there? With his mother?"

"If she was my mother, that's the last place I'd go. I'll say this for her, though. That woman sure knows how to end a conversation real quick."


Early the next morning, Tressa arrived at her antique shop. She entered at the front entrance. Niles Nelson was already in the front of the store, and he looked at her apprehensively as she passed him. She didn't notice. It was when she got to the back of the shop that she saw Marvin sitting on the bench where he had been sitting the very first time he came to her shop. That stopped her in her tracks.

"What now?" she asked.

He'd been there for some time, sitting where he'd been, beside Ron. He'd shown his badge and forced Niles to let him in.

"I made Niles let me in. I'm sure when I was sitting here before I saw the butt of a gun behind some papers on the shelf under that cash register. Isn't there now. Registered gun?"

"If it isn't there now, how could you prove Ron shot Hal with that gun, if there never was that gun there... because I say there never was a gun there."

"Well, of course, I can't, and Ron never shot Hal with a gun, anyway. Emma told me about the walking cane. That's what he attacked Hal with, and I think that's why Hal's alive. If Ron had shot him with a gun, Hal'd probably be dead. Tressa, Ron shot himself. We found his body early this morning."

She collapsed, falling to the floor as if he'd hit her on the head with a weapon. He stayed there long enough to be sure she got help. He walked away from her shop feeling not much compassion for her. He had, after all, been sitting there on that bench for some time with tears on his cheeks, feeling sorry for Ron, for himself, and he had no feelings, nothing, left for Tressa.

At home, he remarked to Frank his conversations with people were getting shorter and shorter.

It was nice of Niles Nelson and his wife and their pastor to go tell Hal the news of Ron's death. Niles told others, later, it was like seeing a light go out in Hal's eyes.

"When I mentioned the gun, Pop, she wouldn't look at me."

"Maybe she thought he'd go kill his father?"

"All I know for sure is she knew that gun was missing. I'd bet on that. Soon as I mentioned the gun, her eyes slid away from me."

Emma had stepped out onto the porch off her second-floor bedroom that early morning with her coffee, enjoying whatever little coolness the day was going to provide. Because she was on the upper level of her home, she could see farther, all the way down the field rows to the spot where a road divided the farms of Reegie and Shaggy. There she could see headlights, and then she could tell that vehicle was white, as was Ron's convertible. That caused her to exit her house and go running through the soy beans across the field to his car, her bathrobe flapping against her legs as she ran.

Ron's body was behind the wheel. He'd shot himself in the head. He'd left a note for her on the car seat, telling her he was sorry, that Scrambler's body was in the trunk, and would she please bury Scrambler somewhere on her property. There were also these words: *I love you dearly. You know that. Sorry.*

She opened the passenger side door, and, for a while, she sat beside him, cradling his upper body against herself, weeping. Later, with no tears she called Marvin. and he'd decided to tell Tressa, leaving Thalia out of it this time.

Alone, that evening, Emma dug a wide, shallow hole in her flower garden, and that was where Scrambler got buried.

Marvin was having a lazy weekend morning. As Frank and he talked, they sat in a glider on the porch, lazily swinging back and forth. It slowly became apparent to Marvin something new had been added—this pleasurable thing he was sitting on, matter of fact.

"Where'd this come from?" Marvin asked.

"Thalia says when it gets raining again, we can't sit under the tree, so she got it."

"What? Listen, now, when she starts furnishing—"

"Mighty nice place for taking a nap."

"She hates me, and you're letting her buy porch furniture?"

"You know, the crows are acting funny. Wonder if it means rain."

Lou felt it was such a shame, Hal changing so much for the better and never being able to live a better, stronger life. *Well, he almost made it.* That was what Lou thought. He went to the garden shed, and he found the ax just where he'd put it, wrapped up, under a potting table, not a bit of blood on it. That ax never killed Scrambler, he told Geraldine.

Lou went to the spot where Thalia said they'd found the dog, and then he noticed some blood on the road. Scrambler died on the road, he felt sure. Somebody might have pulled the dog into the lane, but that somebody wasn't Hal Gesler.

When the rains came, the blood would be washed away.

*So this is what happens when love fails children and parents*, Lou thought. Maybe it was a good thing he didn't have any children, after all. For some time after Ron's funeral, Lou would have nightmares, re-living the evening he and his brother saw the tail lights of their father's car as he left them, never to be heard from again. When he went to the hospital to see Hal, he could tell Hal didn't care about anything anymore. Maybe, he thought, you can almost tell how soon they'll be dying; it is so obvious, the way they look, the broken-hearted ones.

The way Hal looked.

Then came the morning he noticed Geraldine coming away from the shed. Curious, he went to look, and he found she'd been watering the marigolds. Those plants were certainly tall and needed to be planted. Sighing, he took the flats out to the rose garden and, on his knees, began planting them. Shortly after he started, Geraldine showed up, and she joined him in planting them. She said nothing, and neither did Lou, but after that got done, somehow he felt better.

He wondered if Thalia would ever know the truth about the dog's death, but somehow, it didn't seem important anymore.

Ron Gesler was buried on a Friday in Verde's historic cemetery. That section of it dominated by Geslers included his grandparents and great-grandparents, and his aunts and their families. It was well known among the mourners that Ron's death was no accident, but that wasn't discussed. Perhaps the feeling was that if it wasn't acknowledged, it wouldn't exist—a suicide in the family.

Joe and Shaggy, Reegie and Emma, Marvin and Frank stood apart from the others. It was as if they'd been cast aside, fingered, as the few keeping the others from the wealth they felt they deserved. Thalia was seated, stoic. But as the cars left the cemetery, Marvin could see she was weeping.

As the funeral ended, it became cloudy. Talk was, rain might be coming.

Emma later wrote in her journal:

*Ron wanted parents to love him. It wasn't his fault they didn't know how. I read somewhere George Burns sometimes went into the cemetery to sit on a nearby bench and talk to Gracie. There needs to be a bench there, then, for Ron.*

Davis had a talk with Marvin, and now it was time to have another talk with Thalia.

"Why me?" he'd asked Chief Davis.

"Well, it's about Tressa, and she's at Thalia's place now, and you helped before, about Tressa, so… it's just a conversation, that's all. See what you can do. I hear it's tight feelings there now…"

He wanted to see Geraldine first, so that's where he went, to the kitchen, with his hat in his hand.

Tressa hadn't attended Ron's funeral. Instead, she'd been sedated heavily, kept in her bedroom. Now, she was getting up and moving about, and Geraldine was suffering because of that.

"I have to give Thalia some news, Geraldine," he said at once. "Is she here?"

"Good news… or bad news? We could use some good news here."

"Probably good. She'll tell you about it, not me."

Geraldine was grumpy. "I have to deal with her," (and he knew she meant Tressa), "and everybody else steers clear. She's at the Realty office (and he knew she meant Thalia) with Emma. I bet they go to the diner for lunch, won't come *here*, I bet."

At the Gesler Realty Office, he could tell he wasn't welcome. There was an awkward silence when he came in.

"It's important or I wouldn't be here," he said quickly, and he looked at Emma as he said it.

"I don't want you to leave," Thalia said to Emma. Emma looked at Marvin inquiringly, eyes asking for help.

"It's fine with me if Emma stays." He was tired of hot weather and of being helpless. To hell with it.

He'd never been in the Gesler Realty Office before. He was in a circular open greeting area at the front, and he could see secretarial stations and some enclosed offices farther back. There was before him a large table with chairs around it, and it looked as if Emma and Thalia had been having lunch there.

There wasn't an answer so he sat down, ignoring the napkins

98

and other paper there, and, slowly, he took off his hat.

"Well, Thalia, please sit down." Her eyes got a little bigger, and she did sit down, and so did Emma after a moment's hesitation.

"Last night, your father died in the hospital. I'm guessing you expected that. Arrangements will have to be made for his funeral, but that's not why I'm here. Seems Hal's banker talked first thing today with Hal's lawyer, and that fellow talked with Chief Davis, and that's why I'm here to talk to you.

"Just listen, so I don't have to come say all this twice. When Hal married Tressa, all the house and business, all the whole works, stayed in his name, but he had a will, and Tressa was in it. Two years ago, he changed his will. He cut Tressa out of it entirely. He left everything to his children. Now Ron's gone, that means only you.

"But there's two things a little complicated. One is Tressa's been using the house as a sort of business storeroom, and you know that. It's loaded with her antiques, and every now and then, she'll add one or take one out to sell. You know that's true. The will means you inherit the house and all its contents. *All its contents* means unless Tressa can come up with some receipts or bills of sale or something or other, you will have complete say, have ownership, of all her stuff in the house."

He let that sink in for a moment. "You need to have that lawyer with you when you let her know that."

"What's the other thing? You said more than one," Emma asked.

He was fiddling with his hat. "And I don't think Tressa needs to know this from the banker. Once Hal started being drunk so much, he forgot, let's say, when his banker told him things, sent him statements. He just sort of assumed, once he got bad news from the bank that all the news would be bad. I'm guessing he didn't even open a lot of bank mail. Fact is, Hal had two things he probably forgot he had. One is a safety deposit box that needs to be opened—I hope you can find the key to it—and the other is an account held in trust for him, coming from his maternal grandmother. Banker will have to talk to you about those things. Chief Davis seems to think it might be a substantial amount of money. You'll have to go see the bank on these things, Thalia."

Thalia sort of slumped in her chair, head lowered. Then she got up, and Emma and Marvin watched as she went into an adjoining office and shut the door.

He felt the need to say something. Still seated, still hat in hand, he spoke to Emma. "For years, Tressa's treated her pretty bad. A lot of people would be saying, 'Whoo-Whoo, now it's pay-back time.' I knew before I came here, that wouldn't be how she would react. She'll probably let Tressa go on thinking nothing has changed. Help her. God knows, I can't. Talk to Geraldine about all this. Maybe she needs a good stiff drink with my dad. I can't guess. Please, just don't leave her alone, Emma."

At first, a few days later, he thought there were only six people attending Hal Gesler's funeral. Tressa was back at Rosemont now, and she didn't come to Hal's funeral. Lou and Geraldine were there, and the Nelsons and their pastor, and himself. Then he noticed Thalia was there, standing apart, back from the others, as if she preferred being alone.

He instinctively headed in her direction, until he saw how her body stiffened. It was as if she were steeling herself for some kind of attack. He stopped, backed off, put his hat back on, and left at once after the ceremony ended. He was going to try to forget her.

Every evening, after he came home, it helped if he had a

drink. That seemed to help.

A few days later, when he came home from work, he found a joyful Frank sitting on a new sofa in the living room. Frank declared Thalia sent this because when it got cold, they couldn't sit under the tree or on the porch, so this was for sitting in cold weather. Inside, that is.

"How am I supposed to forget her if I have to sit on this sofa?" he asked Frank.

"Oh, there's no harm done. Look, more than one person can sit here. And it can be a good place for a nap. Can be close to the fireplace."

He tried to keep other things on his mind. "You keep forgetting she's not on our side, Pop."

He knew she was sitting and talking with Frank now and then, missing having a father, borrowing his. If he ever got a chance to speak with Thalia, to really talk, to tell her what he thought was important, maybe he'd be able to reassure her. In his imagination, the conversation would always go in his favor:

*You know you're not alone. In time, things will be in your favor, and there's Lou and Geraldine with you, and all your friends, and Dad and me, all of us. We're here for you. Skittles might even have more puppies.*

*You're lucky. You have a dad. But you're against me—*

*Well, maybe not so much as you think. Things will work out, you'll see. Let time and nature work on it.*


Manfred Richter's company got started because one of his family men had served with Rommel and the 15th Panzer Division in Africa. That is, till 1943, when Rommel ran out of fuel. When Rommel returned to Europe, so did the Richter who was Manfred's relative.

That Richter came back with health problems. For various reasons, he'd lost his hair in Africa, and he also had breathing problems. Nothing could be done about the hair, but his family tried improving every respirator they could get their hands on to help him. Eventually they began producing industrial respirators, forming their own company. When some of the family worked on airplanes, they began making parts for airplanes, including propellers. They became a corporation, a large and profitable one. And now they made lots of other parts for aircraft, including parts for jets. And, of course, they still made respirators.

Their success was partly due to the fact Manfred and his son, Ernst, who headed that corporation, were a couple of smart men. Their profit lay in great part in America, so an American plant, in addition to the one in Frankfurt, made sense. The land they wanted should be flat, rural, and close to air traffic. An American Realty company had joined them in searching for the right place, but Manfred didn't care one way or the other about that. It was the plant he cared about. He made the decisions. Ernst was young, unmarried, and as far as Manfred was concerned, a learner.

It fascinated him when he realized the person who had contacted his company was a young female, one representing her father's business interests. He imagined she might be a rather "mannish" sort of female, to have her interests so concentrated. But because he had an active, inquisitive sort of mind, he became interested in what she was offering. Certainly, it didn't take much of an effort to have staff look up what could be found out about that location.

He'd liked what he found out about Verde. It was flat, located close to industry and transportation, yet rural, full of cheap labor. Once he had his interest aroused, it was only a matter of time before he decided he and Ernst should get there in person to see what it was really like. To see what Thalia Gesler was really like, for that matter.

He and Ernst were going to do some traveling, coming to check out the Verde location.

Manfred was sixty-seven and not liking travel. Frankfurt was a chaotic airport, and there was a two-hour delay in New York, but finally they landed at Steeds. They rented a car, and Ernst drove to Verde.

It was raining when they landed, and it certainly seemed to get worse and worse as they drove. They were tired, of course. He was glad his son was driving.

The GPS Ernst was following as he drove didn't have enough information for Manfred. He got out his iPhone and pulled up Google aerial photos. An overhead shot of Verde showed him an alarming thing; you couldn't get into Verde without crossing at least one bridge. The shallow, winding Puncheon River was like a twisting snake, so both getting into and out of Verde, you crossed bridges. There were three of them. Maybe that wasn't such a good thing, but it wasn't the only thing to consider. Manfred was looking at everything as Ernst drove.

He didn't care for airline food even when he was a first-class passenger. When they reached Verde, Ernst slept in the car for a while, and Manfred went into the Verde Diner to get something to eat. He wanted to try some of the local cooking.

He was about to get an earful.

Thalia had set up a meeting for the next day at the middle school auditorium. Everybody knew about it. Once the local population suspected they might all be for sale, there had been a lot of controversy about it for days. In the diner, even though this was the lunch crowd, there were quite a few farmers who planned on staying the night in Verde, just in case the bridges flooded. They didn't want to miss the land sale meeting that was scheduled for the next day.

Presently, Manfred would call Thalia, and she would come lead them to her place. They'd be staying there.

He was led to a very small table in a spot near the clatter of the kitchen, but it didn't matter. He was taking in all the surroundings. A very tall blond approached and asked if he could sit at the table on the other chair there, one of the few seats left. Manfred noted the man looked Germanic. In any case, that was fine, his sitting there.

"I'm Cal Peterson," the man said. He was waving to two others nearby who looked so much like him, Manfred figured they must be family.

"You're a visitor, are you?" Cal asked.

"I'm called Manfred," he volunteered. "Passing through." He didn't want to give his last name. Or say he was from Germany.

"It's crowded today," Peterson said. "People here are for a meeting coming up tomorrow. They might have to spend the night, if the bridges get flooded."

"What kind of a meeting is that?" Manfred asked, as if he didn't know.

"Land sale. So here we are, most everybody who could make it. Well," he added, "here comes some of the worst things about it, for sure." He was looking at the diner entrance door, and Manfred saw three men entering.

The tallest one looked to Manfred as if he could be a cowboy. He was a handsome man, but he had a serious look about him, and as he looked about, he took off his cowboy-looking hat.

"Crap," Cal Peterson murmured. "Marvin took his hat off."

With him was an older man, and Manfred thought that man, even though he was shorter, looked like what he thought an Indian chief should look like. There was a third man, and that one looked like the British sort Manfred dealt with all the time, only, of course, here he would be American.

"His hat?"

"He's Marvin Dorset, and if you know him, you know he means business if he takes off his hat. Or if he puts it on, means the same thing. It's all in the hat, sometimes, with him. That's his father, Frank Dorset, with him. He's an Indian. I don't know who the other fellow is. But I bet it's not good."

Manfred had heard about, read about, Indians, but he'd never seen one. This was fascinating. He had seen a topographical map of this area, with one small portion of it labeled, "Cher."

"What kind of Indians?" he asked.

"Trouble kind, these days, here. Cherokee," Peterson answered.

His food had arrived, but Manfred just sipped his coffee, looking at what Cal Peterson described as "trouble." A waitress found some space at the counter for them, and the three men sat with their backs to the crowd, ready to order. *Cherokee,* then, on that map, Manfred was thinking.

It caused Manfred's hands to jerk so suddenly he almost spilled his coffee when Cal Peterson stood and said loudly, "All right, Marvin, who's the fellow with you?"

It was even more strange that there were scraping and pulling sounds as just about every chair in the diner was turned to face the three men, so as to get a better look, a better listen to them. It was almost a tribal thing. It was electric. Yet the waitresses walked about taking food around as if it were normal.

One voice, anonymous, asked, "Yeah. Has he got something

to do with it?"

For a minute, the three men looked confused, as if they wanted food, not questions, but just as the one called Marvin looked ready to answer, the British-looking one answered for him.

"I'm Doyle Rogers," he said. "I work with some Indian tribes and with the Bureau of Indian Affairs. Yes, I guess I do have something to say... and I'm sorry about that."

There was a moment of silence as the diners digested that word, "sorry."

"Son of a bitch. I knew it." Cal Peterson sat down.

"Well, you see, Frank here can't sell that fifty acres he's got—"

Now there was a troubled murmuring that reminded Manfred of a mud slide he once witnessed, the same sort of moving noise.

"Why the hell not?"

"Is it 'cuz he's an Indian and can't own land or sell it?" Voices without faces were calling out questions.

"No, of course he could buy and sell land, unless he's on a reservation, government land. Indians have been citizens since 1924, the Snyder Act."

An attitude was hanging in the air: It said, *So?*

"Well, see now, citizens must have really liked Frank here's relative back then in 1924, who was living on that same parcel of land way back then. They celebrated his getting to be a citizen by giving that land, as a gift, see, to the Cherokee Nation."

There was an unspoken *What? What's that mean?*

"Well, the land didn't belong to him, but that fellow, since he was the only Cherokee around, he just went on living on it like he always had, and on down till it gets to Frank today. But Frank doesn't own that land, see. It belongs to the Cherokees, and their Council is in Oklahoma."

"They can sell it, then?" Another question from the crowd. Doyle Rogers looked uncomfortable.

"They've got other things on their minds, like diabetes on their reservations. They don't care what white people say. They're not going to sell it."

Now a plaintive voice called out, "Don't they know how important it is?"

What Doyle Rogers said next got Manfred's attention completely.

"I've made it clear to them the location of this parcel of land, sitting so squarely in the center of the available land between the mountains and the nearest cities and airport, is valuable. They don't care."

The old Indian stood and faced the diners. "I can leave right now, if that will help," he said.

The man Marvin said to him, "That wouldn't help, Dad."

"No, wouldn't help," Doyle Rogers added, too.

"Nobody wants you to leave, Frank," some soft voices were saying, and some other voices were adding, "Known you forever, Frank."

"How do we know you're somebody telling us the truth, anyway?" Cal Peterson said.

"I've left some calling cards of mine here by the register. You can check me out any old time. I work in Oklahoma and Wyoming with the Federal Assistant Attorney General."

Cal Peterson asked another question. "Could we use eminent domain on the Cherokees to force them to sell?" Now there were some conversations, for some diners didn't have a clue what that could mean.

"You'd probably spend a lot of money and get nowhere. States are prohibited from using eminent domain against Indian properties."

Peterson exploded. "Well, what the hell, then! We just can't win!"

Doyle Rogers was angry. "Don't take it out on me! I don't make the laws. I'm just here to confirm there's that number 35 U.S. Code 357, to provide what's called 'just compliance' for Indian culture. Indian tribes are considered 'domestic dependent nations.' What that really means is there's no way in hell that land is going to be sold."

One person cried out, "This isn't the way it's supposed to be! One man's place holding the whole thing up! One person isn't supposed to do that. It's not American!"

Manfred saw Marvin Dorset stand up, and he put the worn, casual cowboy hat on his handsome head. "In this country, in this place, my father's world, and mine, rights can't just be pushed aside. In some other places, maybe. But not in this country. Not mine. Not here." The three men left.

Diners began hurrying to finish up, so they could leave and perhaps get across bridges, for it was still raining hard outside. They were going home. Obviously, interest in tomorrow's meeting had fallen off.

Manfred felt as if he'd fallen down some historic time-warp hole. He felt that way, perhaps, because Cal Peterson turned and smiled and said, "Nice to meet you, sir," as he was leaving, as if this sort of thing happened all the time in the diner.

Thunder had wakened Ernst. He came in, sleepily looking for some food. "What's going on?" he asked.

"Well, for one thing, I expect we're going to be here in Verde for a few days, at least."

Manfred couldn't imagine what Thalia was thinking, recommending this area for a land purchase. It meant looking elsewhere in the same state. He'd have to tell her the meeting she planned was out of the question now.

"Boring," Ernst predicted. But when Thalia came to lead them to her place, he quickly changed his mind. Ernst was attracted at once to the beautiful blonde. Manfred, on the other hand, though he was pleasantly surprised at what he saw when he met her, wondered how he could tell her the meeting she had planned wasn't going to happen.

It had rained all night. Now it was early, and there was a pounding on Frank Dorset's door. Marvin came out hastily, wearing his boxer shorts and his open bathrobe, the ties to the robe flailing in the air behind him. Doyle Rogers appeared from out of the extra room behind him. Frank Dorset, who had spent the night snoring on his new gift sofa, was also awake.

Surely it must be an emergency of some kind.

It was an angry Thalia, wearing rain gear.

"You ruined it! You ruined the meeting! Now there can't even *be* a meeting!"

"Wait now! That got messed up in 1924—"

"Phooey!" she exclaimed. She struck at him with her fist. He caught her hand and held it against his heart, his bare chest.

"You were against me the whole time, and you knew what you were going to do the whole time!"

"No, now, Thalia, I didn't know for sure he could even come—"

"Phooey!" she said again, and she jerked her hand away from him. She went stomping off the porch to her car.

He called out to her, "Thalia, we just went in there to get

something to eat. I swear…"

He plodded back into the house, the ties to his robe trailing along damply.

"Can't even get something to eat without trouble. What time is it?"

Doyle turned to look at the clock on the wall near the fireplace. "It's five thirty," he said.

"Can't even *sleep*. And I have to get up and go on duty at seven, so what's the use of trying to go back to sleep?" Marvin stood, overwhelmed, adding, looking at Doyle sadly, "And now she hates me."

"Don't look at me," Doyle said, "I'm divorced."

Frank Dorset, awakened from his sleep on his sofa, lifted his head, looked at them, and laughed.

"Sonofabitch, Sonofabitch," Marvin murmured, until he finally fell asleep again. At home, in her room on the first floor, her guests sleeping upstairs, Thalia tossed and turned for a while thinking hard thoughts about Marvin. But at last, as she finally fell asleep, she remembered seeing, pounding on, Marvin's bare chest. His very masculine, muscular chest.

It rained for most of the week. Geraldine was in her glory, cooking for these two foreigners, one of whom was delighted with every local dish she provided for him to try. She gathered enough compliments to keep her heart warm for at least three winters. With Tressa back in Rosemont, and these two as guests, Geraldine was in Heaven.

Ernst spent his time trying to get and keep Thalia's attention, but she was listening only to what Manfred said he required. Once she understood what Manfred was looking for, during the following days, she borrowed Joe's Chevy Monster truck. She was location-looking, scoping around. Joe's truck could handle back roads, no matter what the conditions were. Thalia was comfortable driving it. She could haul herself up to get into the driver's seat as easily as she once, in her teenage years, mounted horses to ride at a nearby stable

Manfred took one look at Joe's vehicle and immediately wanted to ride around with her. They found a stepladder and managed to get him up into the cab. He looked like an excited child peering out the window when Thalia drove off with him each day.

Her ambition was so intense she actually found property that suited Manfred just fine. He was thrilled with his ride in Joe's vehicle, and he bought the land situated near Rosemont, right off the bat. An unhappy Realty company, seeing limited acreage, withdrew from the sale, but Manfred cared not. He had what he wanted. Later on, when the plant opened, he'd need some homes for some of the executives and specialists he'd be bringing in to run and hire for the plant. Thalia could be looking for those houses.

Meantime, Ernst and he, to get the plant built, would be going back and forth. He and Ernst would take turns traveling and staying between Germany and the United States. Manfred wanted the plant to be in production sometime the following year. He left for Germany, scheduled to return to Verde the next month, pleased with himself... and with Thalia.

Thalia celebrated getting a large commission from the sale of the land in an unusual way. She decided she needed to buy a chair to match the sofa in Frank's house.

Marvin had been stunned, earlier, when he saw the sofa. Now, it looked as if there would be more coming. It would be easy to give up, but when he visited Shaggy and Emma, he asked for help.

Perhaps in response, Emma invited both Marvin and Thalia for lunch, but Ernst was in town, staying at Thalia's place, of course, and Thalia couldn't come. Or perhaps she wouldn't, if she suspected Marvin would be there, for she was still angry— not at Frank, but at Marvin.

Lou kept Marvin informed about what was happening in the house, with Ernst being there, hanging around Thalia.

"Oh, he's after her, no doubt. He's nice enough, but he probably never had to do much. Better at kissin' than liftin', you know what I mean."

That piece of news had Marvin taking off his hat and putting it back on his head several times as he walked to the squad car.

This time it was worse. It was Frank who broke the news Thalia wanted to buy a chair to match the sofa. The excuse was the sofa looked funny there all by itself, except for the few other pieces they had there in their sparsely furnished house.

This time, Marvin called Thalia. He wanted to be along for the purchase. His home, his father, you know? Startled, she said yes.

Ernst wasn't pleased with the addition of Marvin. That became apparent in about five minutes. When Ernst mentioned a furniture store in Rosemont where they could get a stylish chair, Marvin leaned up against his squad car and tugged at his hat. He said he didn't think they'd be going there to buy a stylish chair that was to go into Frank's house.

"Dad needs a chair that's comfortable, not one that's stylish," he said.

Ernst rose to the occasion with what he knew was an advantage. "I thought if I'm paying for it, I could choose the proper sort of chair," he said.

Now the hat came off, its brim twitching in one hand. "That's just it, see. You're not to be paying for it. If it's a chair for my home, I'll pick it out, and I'll go buy it, and I'll pay for it, and that's the way it is. And that goes for every other thing, too." The hat was being twirled.

"Okay, fellow," Ernst declared, and he pulled away, laughing. Thalia, seated beside him, wasn't laughing. She looked thoughtful. Ernst and she spent the morning together, and they had lunch together, but no chair was bought by them, not that day.

Inevitably, one day when Marvin got home, he found Frank enjoying his new recliner.

"Don't you say anything about this one! This is the best one yet! I bet Thalia had to go all the way to Steeds to get this!" Frank Dorset was excited, pleased.

"I'm not saying anything," Marvin responded. "Just sitting here minding my own business. If you like it… and I can see you do… I'm not going to say a single thing bad about it."

He and Shaggy had bought it at a furniture store in Verde and had it delivered while Frank was out pulling onions.

It made him smile to see how Frank liked it. Of course, it was going to be a different story when Frank thanked Thalia for it… if he ever did that… and found out it came from Marvin— but he liked watching Frank being joyful. He noticed how his father sighed when he got his aching left leg propped up comfortably on that new recliner.

In the meantime, the summer was careening into August. What the drought did to farmers, the flood had made worse. It hadn't been the kind of flood that carried off cars. This was just the kind of creeping water that came and stayed and stayed. The only thing that really liked it was roses. Geraldine had been cutting blooms every day.

And now, with the water gone, farmers tried to deal with what they had left. It wasn't much. For many, their orchards were the only money maker they would have that year.

Marvin had called Shaggy before, getting her to help him pick out a chair. Now he called her again, to see if she knew of someone who could fix two holes in his jacket.

"Holes? What kind of holes?"

"Bullet holes. I'm fine. I just need my jacket repaired."

"Bring the jacket here to me, and I'll get it fixed," Shaggy told him.

Marvin was still feeling a little wobbly, but he didn't want to tell Shaggy. He had no idea whether his jacket would "speak" to her. There was one hole where a bullet went into the side of the jacket, and another hole was where it exited, both holes on the same side. When he had turned away as fast as he could, that one bullet must have gone through a fold of his moving jacket; that, at least, was what he decided. He'd felt that bullet pass so near his torso.

It was weird. He'd been sent to make contact with a snitch Davis always used, letting that person know the sheriff wanted a phone call. It was supposed to look like he was asking about a drug deal that had gone wrong at that corner where such things sometimes happened.

A car was parked near him, and he saw a hand with a gun come out of the driver's window. He felt that shot as it went through his jacket. He called in what he saw of an out-of-state license number as the car sped off.

Afraid to check to see whether he'd been shot—not wanting

to know till he was where he could get help—he had driven back to the station feeling shaken.

As soon as Shaggy clicked off from Marvin, she called Emma, who was at the Realty office with Thalia. Thalia was on another phone, talking to Ernst, who'd called, as he did nearly every day.

"Guess what?" Shaggy told Emma. "Marvin got shot."

Emma, on the receiving end of that, said out loud, "Thalia, Marvin got shot!"

Emma didn't expect what happened next. Later she told Shaggy, "Thalia turned white, and she hung up on Ernst. She wanted to know if Marvin was dead or hurt, and she was ready to cry. I said to her she should call him at the station and find out."

"Did she?"

"Hell, no."

The two women shrugged helplessly. There was nothing to be done to help when people were so stubborn.

September limped into October. It was amazing how quickly people forgot the land deal and the meeting that never happened. Hard feelings once roiling through the town and countryside were put aside as neighbors and old friends helped each other as best they could.

Shaggy got an idea for Halloween. "Let's us women go trick or treating with the Peterson kids," she suggested. "Thalia, too. She'll go for that. We'll wear some simple get-ups, with masks, and we'll stop at Frank's place. We'll let that be a rest stop for the kids, where they can go to the bathroom. Frank won't mind. There's only four kids. And then Marvin could talk to Thalia, right?"

"He'll probably be on duty that night, when there's vandalism going on, maybe."

"I'll talk to him. He'll have to cooperate, and if we come early as we can, maybe he can arrange his hours so he'll be there. Worth a shot."

"Nothing else works."

Shaggy made sure Marvin knew trick or treaters would be coming, and he should be there, early in the evening, at least, and that Thalia liked licorice, the red kind, so he was to be sure he had that to give out, and then he was supposed to say nice things to her. Emma asked him if he understood all this, and he said he did.

A spooky evening came, and children and parents began making their rounds, trick or treating.

Somehow, it got screwed up. When Marvin put licorice in Thalia's bag, he spoke her name. "Here, Thalia, I know you like licorice," he said.

"How did you know it was me?" she asked, drawing her mask up away from her face.

Her costume was complete, after all, for her hair was covered completely by headdress and scarves, and her body padded, so that she looked like the Queen of Hearts from Alice in Wonderland. How Marvin really knew the costumed being was Thalia would forever be a mystery, but what he said decided it for him was certainly clear enough.

"I know how you walk," Marvin said confidently. Emma could sense disaster, and she was inching closer.

"Oh? How do I walk, then?" Thalia asked.

"Well, strong, like. Strong."

"I hope I don't walk like a boy."

"Uh, no, not like that. Sort of like a person in charge."

"No, no. He means you walk with confidence. Confidence," Emma said.

But the damage was done. Later, Thalia said, "Marvin thinks I walk like I'm the boss."

Emma confided to Shaggy, "Maybe she'll have to be boss, because I'm beginning to think Marvin's dumber than cat shit."

The family women cared enough, though, to let Marvin know Thalia was considering going to Germany for Christmas.

Autumn was such a wonder in Verde that year. In spring, the blossoming apple trees were splendid, but autumn this time of year was for the hardwoods to show off, draped as they were in those same swirls of leaves as those they were showering down—where Marvin sat so disconsolate, thinking himself so poor—with all shades of yellow, orange, and red enriching him. . .

"She's got her passport, and she's thinking about it. Ernst has convinced her Germany is some kind of winter wonderland at Christmas. I thought you should know ahead of time," Emma told Marvin.

He didn't say much. Maybe his hands said it for him. Marvin always noticed hands. Once he'd questioned a person whose mouth was saying all the right things, but his hands were wringing one another desperately. Another time, he noticed a woman arguing with her husband as she stood peering into the driver's side of his car; all the while her hand was smoothing, petting, patting the mirror on the driver's side. Unless you're talking to an Italian person, Marvin thought, hands said a lot. In this case, about Germany, Marvin's hands went into his pockets. Nothing he could do about that, and his hands knew it.

Sometimes Marvin would go to the closet where his mom's coat was hanging, and he'd just feel the sleeve of it, as if he were a little guy again, and she could guide him. "If she goes, Mom, I'm afraid I'll never see her again," he said to the sleeve of the coat.

November came in cold and harsh. All that firewood Marvin had chopped was starting to come in handy. Shaggy had another idea, this one for November. "The full moon comes this year right after Thanksgiving," Shaggy said to Emma and Reegie. "We all have fold-up tables. Let's use them at Frank's place for Thanksgiving dinner. We could seat a lot of people in that big main room where the fire place is, and around the corner in the dining room. Joe will take care of the turkey and all of us, including Lynn and Susan Peterson—we'll all make side dishes. We could set it up buffet style, and have one table for beverages, another table for desserts, and it could be fun, especially with that big fireplace Frank's got. He's got a dining table, too. We can add folding tables to that."

"There's one other thing," Shaggy added. "The full moon comes right after that. We don't have to tell Frank or Marvin about it, but we could have some hot food, maybe a lot of the leftovers, too, for them after they do that ceremony Frank's always done for his trees." It was agreed.

Somehow these hardy families had survived a disastrous time. They wanted one really good Thanksgiving.

Thalia suggested Ernst and Manfred would want to come, too, to see what an American Thanksgiving was like, and then it was suggested Geraldine and Lou should come. There would be a considerable crowd there. Manfred's wife was not in good health, but he wondered what an American Thanksgiving would be like, so he joined Ernst for a brief time in November in Verde, disregarding their usual back-and-forths.

"I'm loving this," Shaggy said. "We could take down the folding tables and fold them up on the porch and use them again just shortly after Thanksgiving—for Frank's orchard ceremony."

Thalia had a request, but this one was for right away. "Manfred's heard about Indians. He's never met one, so he wants to come out and have a talk with Frank," she said.

Frank, when he heard about that, said he'd heard about Germans, too, and never met one, so bring Manfred out any old time. "Just come yourself, too, Thalia, and we'll have some hot tea and cookies."

Marvin wasn't so sure of this meeting. He made certain he would be hanging around that afternoon, just in case. This better not be treating his father as if he were part of some side show. As if they were displaying his Indian dad for fifty cents a photo. Marvin was puffed up, feeling a little indignant.

He wasn't feeling well these days, anyway. He'd had several dreams about Ron. In those dreams, he and Ron were elementary school guys again, and he realized his mind was re-playing the times they'd been "soldiers" under Frank's walnut tree. In his dreams, Ron's young face was laughing at him. He was wearing a GI helmet too big, sort of crooked on his head. The young dream Ron was telling Marvin they would have to get someone new to play being the enemy, because they, the two of them, were always to be together fighting on the same side. Marvin would flounder to wakefulness. And he would be a little frightened by those dreams, because in them, while he was a part of them, he could even smell newly cut field grass, the smell of that, and it made him suspect he'd been in some real place, seeing some real Ron.

Even in the daytime, he'd been feeling unsteady. Once, at the diner he'd suddenly yielded to the urge to leave, standing and saying aloud, "How could I have let that happen to you? How could it have happened?" When alone in his office or in his unit, he'd weep, not knowing when that urge would come upon him.

The two old men sat under the walnut tree at first, but then they got up and walked into the orchard. It was clear they were getting along just fine.

For a while, standing nearby, Marvin was alone with Thalia.

"Where's Ernst today?" Marvin asked her.

"He's at the house or at the Realty Office. Manfred and he sort of came together for part of this month, and there's some phone calls—business has to get done."

He tried not to stare at her, but at last he faced her and spoke directly to her, taking in her flowered skirt, her slender legs, the white top with its rolled-up sleeves, her fingers at her throat.

"I've heard you're considering going to Germany for Christmas." He set the news out there, so she knew he knew. She nodded.

"If you'll accept it, I'd like you to have my mom's warm coat before you go."

"You mean borrow it?"

"I thought of that. I figured it would bring you back here to return it. But that's your decision about where you live. Not mine. No, for you to please keep, because in case you might end up there, I'd feel better if Mom's coat was with you. It would be something of mine looking after you. I'll get it cleaned, though I don't think it's dirty. Thanksgiving, you can take it with you then. Will both of them be here for Thanksgiving?"

"I think so. But I'm not going to stay in Germany, Marvin. It would just be a visit."

He was quiet then. Maybe it would be better to just give up

on everything.

"Are you all right, Marvin?" she asked.

Perhaps she was noticing how he was looking wistfully at the walnut tree where he'd played as a child.

He might actually have whispered it to himself when she and Manfred drove away: *"Don't go. Please don't go off to Germany. No, I'm not all right. I need you."*

Frank said the two men had a nice conversation.

"Do you have an Indian name?" Manfred had asked Frank.

"I do. It's *Boy Who Remembers His Horses.*"

"Tell me about your horses. Why don't you have them now?"

Frank laughed and shook his head. "I never had any horses."

"Huh!" Manfred said, shaking his head in disappointment.

"What does *your* name mean?" Frank asked.

They were walking along between rows of apple trees. Both the two men and the apple trees were gnarled with age.

"Never thought much about my first name. Maybe it means there was a man, and his name was Fred. My last name means "judge."

"Were you ever a judge?"

"No, not even once."

"So much for names, then," Frank commented.

They talked about wives, too, and how they both had one child, a son.

They both had been lucky in love. Lucky in life, so far at least, and comfortable with each other.

"My wife isn't in good health," Manfred said. "She hopes Ernst will marry soon and have children so she can see that happening while she's still around. So far, I haven't seen anybody I want my son to marry… till I met Thalia. She would be perfect."

"Well, you can't have her," Frank said quietly.

"Isn't that up to her?" Now Manfred's eyes were open wide, seeing a stern resolve, even though it was softly spoken.

"Yep, it is, but the day will go to us, me and Marvin, because she knows something you don't know. Maybe my son doesn't know it yet, but she sure does. She knows we need her more than you do. Anyways, I've heard tell the men from Europe aren't so faithful to their wives. They have other women on the side. We two here, me and Marvin, we're more faithful than most, and the need for her is greater here."

Later when Frank told Marvin about the conversation, Frank said, "That old German man looked at me kind of funny when I told him that. But I'm telling you so you know what we talked about. He didn't come to see an old Indian, Marvin. He came to look at you."

"That's not making me feel so good, Dad. I mean, if all I have to offer is being faithful, that's not a lot."

"You worry too much," his father said as he went into the house. "She knows all about it. Women do, you know."


Finally it was Thanksgiving, and everyone was arriving at Frank's place.

The three dogs were delighted to see there were children present, and the dogs stuck with them. "Oh, they're protecting the children," Thalia said.

"Nah. They think they're kids, too," Joe's gravel voice replied. "We had some wild hogs on the place a while ago, and those three dogs made the hogs so miserable, running at them, the pigs left. I think the dogs wanted to play with them. Shaggy says they were trying to figure out what they were. Nobody minds they're here with us, I hope."

Geraldine and Lou arrived with her best cooking, and she wanted to sit near Manfred. The men set up the ham, the turkey, gravy, stuffing and potatoes on the counter in the kitchen. The plates were there, too, so that's where everyone took their plates and started off, going next to the tables where there were all the side dishes and cranberry sauce. One table was for tea or coffee, and the final table was for desserts, some of those old favorites everyone liked. It was a sumptuous feast. Marvin and Joe took turns carving the turkey and slicing the spiral ham.

A couple of things were most pleasing. Cal Peterson's car had a problem at a bridge, and Joe's monster vehicle came to the rescue, pulling Cal's car out of a ditch. All those old angers about land were gone. Thalia had a holly tree at her place, and she'd brought some holly with her in a simple low container. She put that on the fireplace mantel, and when she did that, Marvin saw what her hand was doing, how it was acting, going pat, pat, smooth, smooth on the fireplace with its fire glowing below its mantel.

It was when Manfred and Ernst sat down that Marvin got a big break.

Shaggy had Manfred sit with Geraldine and Lou beside him, facing Thalia across from him. And, since the ladies had given up trying to arrange much for Marvin, they put Thalia with Marvin on one side of her and Ernst on the other.

It was seating not much to Ernst's liking. He was frowning when he saw the arrangement. Perhaps he didn't like having any competition for Thalia's favor and conversation. He had, after all, exchanged some time in Germany to be sure he would be in the United States in November and in Germany in December. He had plans for Thalia in Germany in December. He was glad to come for this occasion, but he'd been looking forward to private time with Thalia.

As Shaggy showed Ernst where he was to sit, she said to him (and everyone heard her say it), "Here, Ernst, now you sit here next to Astrid." She made it worse when she got so flustered about having said it.

"Oh, gosh, I don't know why I said 'Astrid.' I meant for you to sit here by Thalia, of course. Forgive my mistake."

There was a silence, for everybody there except Manfred and Ernst knew that with Shaggy, there never was a mistake. There was an "Astrid" somewhere.

As a matter of fact, there certainly was. Astrid was a past lover of Ernst's. Back in Germany, he'd rekindled that relationship, at least temporarily, and he'd been in bed with Astrid not so very long ago. He had been thinking of her earlier, and now Shaggy hit on that. He didn't know how that could have happened.

Everyone looked in his direction, and his face flushed red with embarrassment. He was caught sitting next to one person, thinking of someone else. Thalia was facing Manfred, and she couldn't help herself; Ernst had been seeking her company so much, she said aloud, "Who's Astrid?"

She was looking directly at Manfred, and she could tell at once Manfred knew who Astrid was. No doubt about it. As a matter of fact, Manfred also knew that while Ernst had been back in Frankfurt, he'd been seeing Astrid again. When Thalia asked her question, Manfred's gaze fell away from her face, away from her question. That said to her, *Yeah, there's an Astrid, but I don't want to tell you about that.*

Reluctantly, inquiring eyes pulled away from Ernst, and Thalia's eyes became downcast. Everyone quietly and happily ate. To hell with whatever that was all about—the food was so good! Private conversations began.

A little later, when everyone was finishing up desserts, Marvin took Thalia away to the closet where Ellie's coat was hanging. "It's not much in style. I know that, but it's soft and warm, and I want you to have it." He ushered her toward it.

He'd noticed how her face fell at the mention of another woman's name.

"About that name, Thalia, it could be anybody, maybe some acquaintance. His social circles are bigger than ours here, because he's got two countries to travel in."

"His face turned red."

"Yeah, well, it did."

Silence.

"What do you remember about your mom, Marvin?"

As was his habit, he reached for a coat sleeve. He held it against his cheek. His eyes grew soft as he remembered the smell of violets, of how Ellie gathered sage and rose petals in her pockets, the smell of those things.

"I remember how she loved me," he said.

Suddenly Thalia was hugging him, and he was hugging her back. He was thinking it, and he almost said it: *Beloved.*

He was kissing the top of her head, holding her tightly against his heart.

"It's as if there's some kind of little silver cord going from me to you, connected." He said that much.

She took the coat off the hanger. She draped it over her arm and moved away, out of the closet. "I do need this coat. I'll take good care of it."

As she left to go back into the main room with the others, he said to her retreating back, "I wanted you to know that, to always know that. I'm somehow connected. Helpless about it. "

Did he imagine it, that for a moment, she stopped, as if she took heed of what he'd said? He couldn't tell, but at least now she knew. She knew now his heart was connected to hers. That if she went away, something of him went trailing along with her.

The next day, it became suddenly and bitterly cold. Marvin sat in his unit, watching, at a point on the highway where he'd been told speeders liked to come careening by, but it seemed to him everyone was staying at home, keeping close by their heat.

Usually, wherever he drove, wherever he sat in his unit, for at least part of the time, Marvin had some Latin or country music playing. It had to have a fast, strong beat, for his mind was wandering, wrapping itself around her. He knew he'd had only a couple of dates (and certainly not with Thalia), and that he'd never danced with anyone. Yet, mentally, many times he allowed himself to be dancing, spinning her—her skirts swirling so he could see her legs, and then drawing her in, close, his arms around her, telling her, "Watch my hips. That will tell you which direction I'm going." He had been doing, mentally, things he never knew how to do, had never done, pushing her out from him, gathering her in—until he'd bring his mind to bear on what he was supposed to be doing, and he would have to quit his "dancing."

But today, this day soon after Thanksgiving, he wasn't doing that. It was a barren day and tonight would be even colder. He was dreading it. It was going to be miserable. A full moon and even colder than it was right now, dammit. dammit, dammit.

There was that full moon. It was as cold outside as Marvin had feared earlier it might be going to be. Frank was bundled up. He was wearing gloves, too, and a cap. Marvin had earlier exchanged the battered old summer hat for a similarly old, battered suede hat. That, with one heavy scarf around his head under the hat and with a lighter scarf wrapped around his neck completed his head gear. He was wearing two coats: one was his own winter coat, and the other was a lined service coat he'd bought for winter police work. And he had thick gloves.

There were a lot of trees out there, and Frank intended to stop at each one.

It was a mystery to Marvin why Frank thought this was a necessary thing to do, this business, every year, but he always went with Frank just the same. He complained this was a crazy thing, but he didn't want Frank doing it alone. "I know damned good and well this isn't some Indian custom," he'd said to Frank. "This is some crazy thing you cooked up on your own." His hands and feet were getting cold even as they began.

It surprised both of them when, at the end of the first row of trees, there was a figure standing, waiting. It startled Frank and made him pause, when he first spied that figure up ahead. He relaxed when he heard Marvin whisper, "Thalia," for then at once he could see that was who it was, wearing Ellen's coat. That wasn't all she was wearing by a long shot. She had on the warmest socks under her slacks, sweaters under that coat, and a wool shawl over her head and shoulders. She'd brought wine, and now she asked Frank if hers could be added to his bucket of wine. "Can I come with you, too?" she asked.

"This is *good* wine," Frank murmured. He always used the cheapest wine for this, figuring trees wouldn't know the difference.

"I've got more, for us to drink," she whispered to him.

Marvin noticed she wore no gloves or mittens.

"This is going to take a while," he warned her. "You're going

127

to be sorry you joined us. You'd better keep your hands deep in those pockets. Thalia, this is going to take at least a couple of hours. You sure you want to do this? "

"Old customs are worth the trouble," she said.

Marvin fiercely thought to himself: *Old customs? Old customs?*

"It *is* kinda cold out here tonight," Frank remarked.

Marvin kept himself from saying out loud the crude thing he was thinking: *Dad, it's colder than a penguin's ass out here, and you know it.* But what he said was, "Yeah, sure is."

They went from tree to tree. Frank dipped a branch into the wine and said some words each time. His message was mercifully brief every time they stopped.

Thalia knew, but the two men did not, that their friends were in Frank's house now, that they were tending to the fireplace, setting up tables, and putting out food. Also, up ahead in the center of the orchard, there were two electric carts waiting for Frank to get to them. Joe wanted some wine he also brought to be added to Frank's wine bucket.

Joe and Shaggy were in one cart, and Emma and Reegie were in the other. Joe wanted the electric carts because they were so silent, but there wasn't any heat in them, so there was mutiny being threatened.

"Are they *ever* coming?" from Emma.

"Joe, it's so cold!" from Shaggy.

"I have to pee!" from Reegie.

"All of you, just shut up! Mom, you shudda gone before we got out here. You're gonna have to go behind a tree." Joe's raspy voice tried to be bossy.

"Are you kidding, Joe?" Emma asked him. "It's so cold, she

wouldn't be able to pull her pants back up."

"There's somebody here in the orchard with us, Joe! I just heard somebody. They just said something! And I have to pee!"

"Me, too!" this time from Shaggy. "I heard that, too!"

"I know I heard somebody!"

"Okay, that's it!" He thought he'd heard something, and this orchard suddenly was uncomfortable. What is so familiar in the daytime isn't that way at night when there's too much silence. Moonlight was making it even worse. The trees were so still it was unnerving.

"Emma, follow me!" he growled at her. His voice still wasn't strong, and this business in the cold wasn't helping any.

He led them up one row of trees, down another, till they came upon Frank and Marvin and Thalia.

When he realized some more very good wine was to be added to his humble bucket, Frank was surprised, and at first he wanted to protest against it.

"Listen, whatever you want about the wine is all right with us. But it's too damn cold out here. Going to drop off the women at the house. They got scared! Get in, Thalia! No argument. You know it's too cold! Let's go, Emma! Frank, I'll be back."

There was a little hesitation on Thalia's part, but Marvin gave her a push, and she squeezed in beside Reegie. The two carts sped away, taking all the females to the warmth of the house.

"Orchard's getting crowded," Frank remarked, continuing on.

Joe returned, keeping apace in his cart with Marvin and Frank as they toiled along on foot. "I'm still not steady about walking. But I want to be here. It is kinda strange out here, you know, at night, like this. Kick it into gear, Frank!"

"Gotta be quiet, then."

Each time he stopped, Frank said the same thing: *Sleep then in peace. I'll be here when you wake.* A low branch touching in the wine. Then on to the next. Stamping their feet to keep some feeling of warmth in them, blowing on their fists and on their curled fingers, the three progressed.

"I wouldn't be doing this for anybody else, Frank. This is torture," Joe grumbled. "I'm not sure I still have feet."

When they finally left the orchard and reached the house, the last tree assured it would be safe to sleep, Joe paused as he got out of the cart. He looked back in the direction of the orchard.

"Huh. There it is again," he said.

"What, again?" Marvin asked.

"Mom said she heard somebody say something. I sort of did, too. And there it is again."

"I don't hear anything. What's it saying?"

"Not sure. Probably something from miles away, on the wind."

Marvin and Frank were surprised, for inside they found a warm fire, food and drink, and friends, all waiting for them. This was a social circle, warm and trusting, based on years of life together, drawn around the fireplace. Someone commented that this event should become a yearly tradition.

"Really? Freezing, listening to bitching?" Joe remarked. "No, thank you. Not happening."

"Nice hat, Marvin," he added sarcastically, noticing Marvin's battered hat on the fireplace mantel where he'd left it when he came in from the cold. "People know it's Frank's old hats you wear!"

"How do you know I don't buy my hats in Steeds?" Marvin countered. Frank glanced at the hat. He smiled.

Marvin put on the service coat he'd worn outside; he took some of the holly Thalia brought with her and headed outside to Ellie's grave. He was pleased when he saw Thalia, wearing Ellen's coat, had followed him out.

"This coat keeps me warm. I'd like to keep it."

"It's yours, then. And you, thanks… my mom loved holly." Thalia came closer.

"I saw how you touched the fireplace," he told her. "Sort of the same way I used to touch that coat. As if you were fond of it, cared about it. It's dawned on me how little I have to offer you. I love this town, and I love this old house. And… I guess you know I've always loved you, even when I was a kid. But Ernst, he can offer you so much more. Maybe what I am isn't enough, not enough for anybody, that's what I've always felt."

"Was your mother happy?"

"Oh, yes."

"Then I think I will be, too." She said that as she went into his arms.

*"Beloved," he whispered.*

Inside, Emma wondered where Thalia could be.

"He went out there to put some holly on his mother's grave. She's out there, too," Emma was told.

"Well, she should come in. It's too cold out there." She headed toward the door.

Now, Cal blocked her way.

"You mustn't go out there right now, Emma. Marvin's took his hat off, so to speak." He smiled suggestively.

It took her a moment to realize what Cal was telling her.

"Oh. Thanks for noticing," she said, smiling back.

"Thanks for listening. Will you join me for a beer? Some of

Thalia's wine?" His eyes were pleading with her as he asked.

"Who's out there in that spooky orchard tonight, besides us?" Joe asked Frank.

"Nobody. Nobody I know of, anyway,"

"Says you, Frank. We heard somebody. I heard something twice. Shaggy!"

He called to her, as she stood talking near the fireplace. "You heard that voice, too, didn't you? What was it saying?"

"What? Oh, yes, I heard that, too." She moved away from the fireplace, toward them, so they could hear her better. "It was a little strange. But I heard what it said. It said 'Good enough, then!'"

"One of those trees was talkin' to you, Shaggy," he teased. She laughed.

"See? I told you," he said, grinning at a startled Frank.

For some time after the last friend left, Frank stood, hands braced against the fireplace mantel, staring into the flames, remembering the woman who had lit up his life for such a short time. He couldn't guess then, couldn't know until later, that outside, just a few yards away, Marvin, with hugs and passionate kisses and beautiful words from the heart, was making damn sure Thalia Gesler wasn't going off to Germany. It suddenly wasn't too cold outside.

Indeed, the next day, she would be bringing Ellie's coat back to its closet, and shortly after that, she would be coming to the house herself. To stay. Marvin would have the bride he loved; Thalia the father she never had; and Frank Dorset would go about whistling, loving again life on his farm.

Meanwhile, outside, now, tonight the orchard was at peace,

At Joe's place, the three Great Danes, left behind this time, were sleeping in a huddled warm pile. They knew, as good dogs do, the best way is to be with those you love, where you love to be, doing what you love to do. Nothing else matters more than those things. For if we live having those things, we have it all.

Good enough, then.


The End

CPSIA information can be obtained
at www.ICGtesting.com
Printed in the USA
LVHW030047260223
740200LV00001B/71